# THE CLEANSING POWER OF FIRE

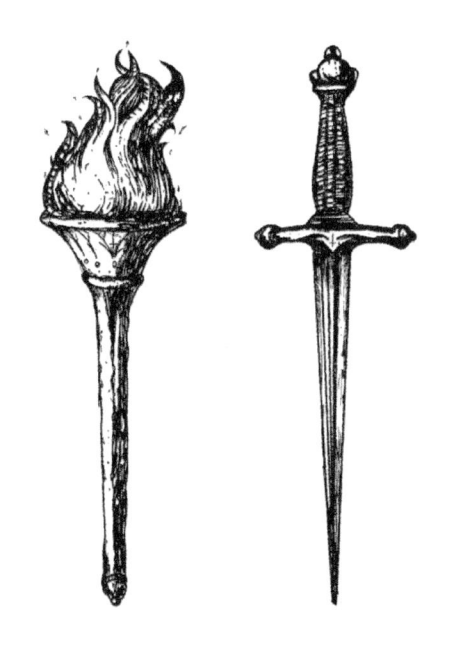

# AN *INFESTED PUBLISHING* ANTHOLOGY

2

INFESTED
PUBLISHING

Artwork by Cut Fingers
Edited and Formatted by Laura Cathcart
First edition 2025

# † CONTENTS †

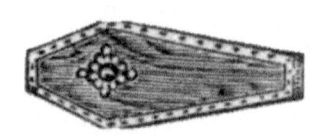

*"Hail, behemoth, spirit of the dark, take thou my blood, my flesh, my skin and walk.*
*Holy behemoth, father of my life, speak now, come now, rise now from the forest, from the furrows, from the fields and live."*

*The Blood on Satan's Claw (1971)*

# VANESSA SANTOS
# BODY OF CHRIST

"It's time for a new story," she said, and she set the town on fire. She had called upon God and saw nothing but flames in her dreams, which she read as prophecy.

"Come, Martha," she said to me, holding out a hand. We were so close to the fire the heat from it made my skin tingle. I thought I had never seen fire burn that bright, spread that quick. She had closed the gates, there would be no survivors. I fancied I could hear them; waking in the night to the smoke, the light from the flames, well before the heat cooked them dry. Waking and wandering out in confusion, confusion turning to panic, then screams, piercing screams that still could barely be heard above the roar of the fire.

I took her hand, what else could I do? She was a saint, risen from the ground to do the Lord's work. We walked away from there, the only home I'd ever known. A curious emptiness, where my sorrow for it should be. While I held her hand, I felt no fear and no sadness.

We reached the next town as the sun was dawning. I remembered her arriving to my town, now surely nothing but cinders, how she walked through the open gates with bare feet, bleeding onto the pavement. How bright she had seemed. How we had taken her in, Father had blessed her before she crossed our doorway as though he was just making sure she was heaven-sent and not a cruel trick. For several nights, she had sneaked into my bed and we would lie still and whisper secrets in the dark, like children. She told me she spoke to God but that I must never tell anyone, not yet. I was jealous then, bitterly. Why had He never spoken to me? The priest's daughter, born in a holy house, raised on communion bread, taking His body into me every week. Why had He never even loved me enough to forsake me – you cannot forsake that which you do not visit, not even once.

She told me stories, at night. She told me of the saints, called them by name as though they were friends she had played with in years past. She told me of the holy book. In her mouth it sounded so different from what Father spoke of. There was so much more hellfire in hers.

It wasn't that long before I felt the restlessness in her. Her visions changed. She stayed out late most nights; sneaked back in through a window she had me keep open for her. I never asked where she went, did not want to hear of how she met God in the dark and danced all night long. She started fidgeting during mass, hands closed into tight fists, her eyes ablaze with something I did not recognize. We'd find her bent over her bible, lips mouthing the words along silently as she read, a furious intensity upon her. Father bent his head at the sight, uttered a prayer, made the sign of the cross. Told us to never disturb her while she communed with God.

Then she waited for night to fall and woke me from a hazy sleep, dragged me outside of town. She walked differently, straighter, poised like a queen. She had done everything while I slept, she had made it so that when she laid down that first flame the whole town would ignite. I did not ask questions. A new story, she'd said, and I knew she had found the holy book lacking, I knew God was telling her to write it differently.

We arrived somewhere new, as I said, as the sky slowly turned golden. It looked a little like flames. I was afraid to let go of her hand. She pulled me along and I fancied her every step caused flowers to sprout from the earth. When I looked back there was nothing there but our sooty footsteps.

They took us in. The new priest blessed us. He looked nothing like Father, yet I looked at him and it all felt the same. I did not know you could change lives like that, slipping out of an old skin and putting another one on. It fit just the same. They gave us water, bade us to wash the ash from our bodies. She washed my feet, kissed each toe as she was done. She was a prophet, beaming at the world with hidden knowledge.

We were given a room and endless kindness. Someone travelled back to check on our burned town. They whispered and wondered about what had happened, made blasphemous little spells to hide over their doorways to keep doom away. I wanted to spit at them for their disdain of God. I wanted to ask them if they had a better one I could trade mine for.

When she left me alone I felt hollowed out. I tried talking to God, too. I tried coming up with new stories myself. We had left our bibles behind. I was not wholly sure what it all meant. Not wholly sure but surely holy.

We sat in the back, at mass. We followed all the rites. The host tasted like ashes in my mouth. I thought of the Easter ashes pressed across my forehead by my Father's hand. She had returned them all to dust, just as God had promised. We had done well to remember. I pressed this knowledge close to me, told myself God's body tasted like His word come to life. I sipped His blood and wished I could feel Him come alive inside me. I watched her as she closed her eyes while taking Him in. She glowed so bright I was sure everyone could see the godliness in her.

Several months we stayed, until the rhythms of the people were imprinted into me, felt like home. My knees took on the shape of the new church floor. I prayed harder than ever before. She was quieter, no longer whispered to me at night. No longer talked of stories at all. I caught her eyes sometimes, and she would smile at me and tell me to be patient. What for, I do not know. For His second coming, maybe, as we were all waiting.

She burned again, for when there is that much of God swimming through your veins it cannot be contained. I almost asked her if this was not yet the new story she wanted, but she took my hand again and we walked on. She was an angel and she would take me to God. For her, even He would swallow whole all the old stories and remake them in her image.

# FLORENCE-SUSANNE REPPERT
# THE UNHOLINESS OF CATHOLIC SLASHES

Solemn faces of watercolor judgement stare down at the casket
from windows held together by wired bones and stained glass
cartilage begging not to be left as broken as that which lies in the
box of pine.

I'd been dreaming of bloody rivers washing down the aisle of a
church.
Cleansing the heels of fellow sinners gathered on opposite sides
of the aisles to collect their penance, or the evidence of crimes
past committed still embedded in my back.

The pews are filled with the still living through it, wondering
where I've gone.
Wondering, how could I leave them to drown in sacrifices never
willing to be made.
Why were prayers shoved against plaster lips sewn up tight from
the inside
Stitched from heart
To throat
To clenched teeth
Not enough to loosen the tongue to ask for help?
Guilt and shame are sisters that swim face down in the clotting
inlet, a reflection to those who dare look and see themselves in
the silent answers.

I'd been dreaming of rotting.

Waiting for a salvation of white light, the end of tunnel wherever
it leads
There must be a somewhere in the cosmos beyond the simplicity
of heaven or hell that exists for someone who kept handing the
knife to those who would say they did nothing to cause this,
knowing the outcome.

But still, hoped for better.

# AMY BOUCHER
# JOHN BARLEYCORN

As soon as I laid eyes on the priest, I knew that he must die. There was something about him that unnerved me, that shook me to my core. It was an uncanny feeling; I was Lot's wife, helpless to its pull. It felt as if he was somehow more than he should be, more than human, and I knew that if I did not hold fast, he would drive me to damnation.

Take the subtle golden hues of his hair for example. Of course, it was seemingly innocuous in the half-light, but, when bathed in the sun's glow, it shimmered endlessly like fields of corn. Then, there were his eyes, his awful, awful eyes… they were too blue, far too blue. He had a stillness about him, a stillness that at first appeared to bestow upon you a kind of grace. But this 'grace' made you afraid to meet his gaze, lest your secret desires and tar black thoughts be realised.

Who was this man? This purported gentleman of the cloth? Who had wandered into the village one day, seemingly unannounced. I had never seen such a preacher like him. I often wondered what profane and ancient knowledge he held beneath that brow. Trickster! He was Astaroth and Moloch, a subversion of all that was holy. He made a mockery of me, and his unrepentant gaze seemed to be burned into my skull. He scorned me with his cheery countenance and that chilling, unwavering stare.

As time went on, my curiosity grew to discontent, and eventually hatred. I loathed him, and somehow knew that he was to blame for all of my previous suffering. The path that I had walked had never been straight forward, but I had always listened to the apostles and walked in faith. However, his torment was too much, and so, I began to avoid the church completely. I couldn't bear to witness this devil, this false prophet preaching the gospel. Religion had been such a previous source of joy in my life, but now it was tainted, there was pestilence and locusts everywhere. Instead, I took to solitude and isolation, convinced it would be my saviour. I turned to the fields and furrows, in hope that the quiet azure solitude would purge my unclean thoughts.

The days slowly melted away, and the priest made himself a prominent feature of the village. Of course, the congregation flocked to him, idolatrous fools, they showered him with platitudes, even invited him into their homes. They were so eager to win the favour of Baphomet that they didn't see how the machinations of his control were unfolding. My hatred in this time only grew deeper, more destructive, and stronger was my resolve. I knew I would be the one to undo him.

It was not long before spring danced across the valley, though it carried with it strange portents and omens of ill. The village, predominately made up of rich arable land was usually drenched in the essence of life at this time, but alas, now it lay barren, devoid of any life or colour. This continued for some time, and soon enough people began to panic, whispering quietly of catastrophe. After this, the days grew drier, little rain fell, and the rivers began to run dry. A general malaise fell upon the population, which mingled with fear and confusion.

I tried to keep a level head and took to recording the event meticulously, keeping an eye out for further signs or presages. I could tell we were at the advent of some unprecedented time, and thus saw it my duty to record the happenings. No crops grew, no sign of life and the colour drained from the vale, leaving darkness, fear, and uncertainty.

Of course, the villagers flocked to the priest, and he tried to soften them with hollow words and a forked tongue. I could see through him though; I understood his deceit. I knew that I would have to be stronger than the rest, I knew that I had to think sensibly. Though I didn't know for certain, I knew in my heart that the priest was to blame. I had to find proof; I had to stop him. I had to do something…however; I was soon to be met with further challenge.

My determination faded on the day that the birds fell. En masse, they danced from the heavens, the delicate hues of their feathers catching the dim light briefly, whispering of hope, before hitting the floor with a resounding thud.

Their once radiant bodies now lay broken, littering the earth. It was a pitiful sight, to see them reduced to such fragile things. They didn't deserve this… they didn't deserve it at all.

Whilst walking through the barren fields, I happened upon a whole flock of them, lying dead beneath the branches. Grief overcame me, my veins and capillaries flooded and burst from the pressure. In that moment I wanted to scream, to curse the infernal beings that had caused such suffering, to drag them up from the depths and destroy them. It was a terrifying, primal feeling. I fell too, my face touching the earth, muffling sobs with my hands. I was an exhausted, broken thing. This was too much, too much. Sitting beneath the dead oak, I wept desperately.

I wanted to restore them, to share my life force. I picked them up, held their small bodies to my chest, and threw them skyward; begging them to take their wings and soar, but they fell,

Fell,

Fell,

And crashed to the ground.

My tears salted the earth, my heart was a chasm now, too black, too black…

He has cursed us.

This vile creature, archfiend, a wolf in sheep's clothing. He brought with him a pestilence, I was sure of it, and it was destroying my home. Without warning, I felt my spirits rise, inflating the space in my chest. There, as I sat upon the tainted earth. I made a promise, to all that would listen, I would fix this mess, I resolved to be its saviour.

I struck at night. Enveloped in the shadows I walked, clad in death.

It is hard for me to describe the look on his face, when he saw me stood over him, smiling. Such terror, such confusion, it was ecstasy! Oh, he had been such a fool; you see, he had not locked his front door, perhaps lured in by the safety of the village.

For two nights previously, I had completed the same ritual, climbing his ancient stairway, softly opening the door to his bedchamber to stand before him. I waited patiently, watching the gentle rise and fall of his chest, edging closer and closer to his bedside. But, on the third night, I moved even closer, so close I could feel his breath against my face...

His eyes opened so gently, looking up. He saw me, smiling.

Quickly I mustered all my strength and struck him, just once, with awesome force. It was enough to knock him unconscious. Here I acted methodically, wrapping his body in his bedlinen. I even covered his face; I couldn't bear to look at it.

With his unconscious state it was difficult to move him, isn't it strange how easily a human can be transformed into a leaden weight. I laboured on however, convinced in the urgency of my noble pursuit, dragging him by the ankles down the stairs.

His shallow breaths infuriated me. I wanted to cave in his skull, right then, in that moment, smash his brains and splatter them across the ground. I wanted to destroy him, wipe him off the face of this world and remove the curse he'd put on me, on us. To leave nothing but a stain as a reminder of his existence but... I breathed deeply. The task had barely begun. I needed to see it through, do it right. There were certain formalities to consider, the birds had told me that, they instructed me the correct way, they whispered promises of rising again, of a second chance.

He started to rouse as soon as we reached the fields. They were still devoid of any growth or crop. The bastard clawed at the sheet like a kitten, weak and desperate. His muffled pleas were music to my ears, urging me forward, driving me on.

When we reached the centre of the field, I slammed his body down, it made a gentle thud. The silence was calming, it promised of new life.

I waited, ignoring his quiet pleas, and breathed in the fading darkness. It would be dawn soon, and we would fix it together. We would make it right again. I could barely contain my excitement.

The gentle rise of the sun felt euphoric as it warmed my skin. My heart was a drum, clattering in my chest but I felt calm, I was where I should be.

It was time. I lifted the sickle and tore at the sheet, revealing his flesh to the light. He was crying now, crying as I laughed with newfound joy. He begged me, oh how he begged in those final moments, his lips laced with false promises, but I was unrepentant. I stood still, smiling as the tears danced down my cheek. I lifted the sickle with purpose and chanted with every fibre of my being.

'I make this vow upon this stubborn ground,
John Barleycorn must die'.

The flames came next. A baptism of holy flame, wrathful and pure, burning up the chaff with unquenchable fire. I consigned him to a second death, the fiery lake of burning sulphur. I became the word of God; my vestiture dipped in blood.

Silence.

My breath was thunder across the land, which was now painted red.

The harvest will come again.

# LYDIA WAITES
# PEG FYFE

## PEG

They run from the wind in these woods, mistaking it for my breath, the whisper of branches for the rattle in my throat. *Witch*, they called me. Ghost, they say today.

LYDIA WAITES
PEG FYFE

## WITSCUN ARMS

Pint of Fyfe, please.

Strong stuff, that.
Bitter as its namesake.

Aye, can't say Peg would be too happy with that as her legacy.

Could've done with one or two
to wash the spoon down.

The men laugh.

Spoon?

She was hung—hanged—either way, it didn't take.
She stuck a wooden spoon down her throat—

Silver, weren't it?

Silver would bend. Poke right through her skin.

I was always told metal.

Either way, the noose couldn't do its job. When they left
her there for dead she took off, neck and whatever spoon
she used intact.

Christ.

'Course, they caught her a few years on, up in those
woods. Strung her up and ran her through with swords
for good measure. No spoon-swallowing could save her
there.

Old wives' tale.

Some details, no doubt. But Peg was real as you
or I.

To Peg, then.

They raise their glasses.

To Peg, and her spoon. Cheers.

Cheers.

Cheers.

## GOODMANHAM GARAGE

The boy gives the barrel a wide berth as he passes the workshop. He tells himself it's because of the smell; the sharp scent of oil emanating from it. His mum would kill him if he got it on his clothes, but his dad's story of the witch and the stable boy still circles his mind.

Peg cornered the stable boy one night, his dad had explained as they were applying a coat of varnish to the workshop doors. Asked him to leave the stable doors open and threatened to flay him alive if he ran his mouth, so—smart lad— he summoned his master to the stable and whispered the witch's plan to the horses for the farmer to overhear. Still, the lad was no match for Peg in the end. Not after her plans were scuppered and she lost half her crew that same night.

What happened? The boy had asked.

She escaped.

To the stable boy.

Well—a painstaking pause as his father applied another lick of varnish—she delivered on her promise.

The boy asked their neighbour, Mags, what flay meant later that day. She'd squinted down at him, asking why he'd want to know a thing like that, and he repeated the story.

That's no story, Mags said, a grim set to her mouth. Peg came back for the poor lad and flayed him head to toe. But your ears are too young for this.

I'm almost ten, the boy said. I know the rest of it.

Mags regarded him for a moment before relenting. Skinned like a peeled sock, he was. An oyster shucked. And where he crawled afterwards no grass would grow; no life where he lay bleeding.

The boy scoffed around a lump in his throat.

That's not true.

Maybe so, Mags said. But that woman was a witch alright, in name and in nature.

The boy doesn't believe the part about the grass—load of rubbish, his dad would say, superstitious old bat—but he can't shake her words from his mind. An oyster shucked.

He spotted something floating in the tractor oil this morning. A rag, he told himself, regarding the bucket again, but he had thought it was the stable boy's shed skin staining the oil red, discarded there and floundering still.

Old tractor diesel, his dad had explained when he asked about the oil's red hue. A warning finger raised. Don't get it on you.

The boy avoids the bucket after that, regardless. Imagines the stable boy's hollow hands reaching for him when he passes it, sure that if he were to glance over its rim some eyeless face would stare back at him.

At night he dreams of the empty skin crawling from the bucket and dragging itself across the fields, a trail of blooded oil in its wake and Peg pursuing it still.

LYDIA WAITES
PEG FYFE

## FIDDLE-DRILL FARM

*Kids*, the man mutters. The amount of times he's had to rush outside when they've set the dogs barking, thoughts of massacred hens or worse, only to find a group of village kids poking about the stables or on the bald patch of land at the edge of his fields.

He shushes the dogs. There's nobody around, but he's sure that if he were young enough to jog past the stables he'd glimpse some breathless gaggle sprinting off down the hill.

They're harmless, his daughter said when he talked about putting up a sign, some more fencing.

Tell that to my knees, he'd said. And it's my property.

She gave him a look that rightly called him an old git.

Still, he resents having to leave his chair by the fire and tramp across the farm on nights like this. The dogs won't give him any peace until he does, nor that nagging part of his mind that's always awake to the farm's needs.

He casts the dogs in torchlight as they sniff at the plant pots framing the porch. He may as well check on the horses while he's out here. The kids never go past the gate, but he knows the stables are an object of interest for them; especially this time of year, hopped up as they are on ghost stories and bravado. He remembers the tales. He'd been told them himself, had told them to his own children to keep them from wandering too far: *Peg will get you if you're out past dark.*

The locals have decided his stables are the ones where that young stable hand worked, and the patch of dead land blighting his furthest field where Peg finally reaped her revenge. He knows for a fact the lad didn't work here. That it all happened up by Kilnsea, or so he'd always been told, but the villagers don't want to hear that. Their children take it in turns running from the bald patch of earth to the stables in the dark, jumping out on the runner or scarpering before they make it back.

He reaches the stables, stroking the old mare's neck. The dry patch of grass is just that; brought about by a spill of oil or the sheep gathering there on a night. Worn down, even, by the parades of children across his land. His neck prickles as he scans the dark fields, though. Easy to see shadows in this light. Easy to recall the detail of that story he can never quite shake: that the stable boy never screamed as he was skinned. Not 'til they reached his palms and the soft soles of his feet.

Degloving, they call that.

The farmer pictures a body stripped of flesh, dragging its way through the dirt. A pulp of a person. The word doesn't feel strong enough to fit the crime.

He shivers, turning back to the light of his porch. If there were such a thing as curses, he thinks, every drop of blood that spilled from that boy would surely curse the ground.

LYDIA WAITES
PEG FYFE

## GOODMANHAM GARAGE

He came running in the other night, scared out of his wits, she says. Talking about that stable boy. I wish you hadn't filled his head with all that.

I only told him the watered-down version! It's those boys he plays with, they've this game they play where they run from him, or from Peg. It's harmless fun.

I bet Mags's been running her mouth at him, she says. You know how she is. She had me running from my own shadow as a girl.

Can always trust Mad Mags, he snorts.

Don't call her that.

Out of her tree, she is.

Still. I don't want her giving him nightmares too.

He'll be alright. He strokes her arm. It's just kids being kids.

## NO. 12, WICSTUN WAY

What was that noise?

>Why, are you scared?

Shut up.

>The cat, probably. Wanting to
>be let in.

>I don't know, it's that time of year…

>Don't start.

Start what?

>His ghost stories.

>It's not a *ghost* story. Kind of.

The younger girl doesn't want them to call her a wimp.

Go on.

>Once a year—don't laugh. Once a year, on the
>day she died, Peg Fyfe comes down from
>Skelfrey Woods and wanders the streets…

What for?

>I don't know. Witch stuff. Hexing people.
>Stealing kids.

>My mum said she wasn't a witch. She was just a
>criminal.

        Trying the locks, then. To steal things. Anyway,
on this night, the stable-hand she killed comes
out from wherever he crawled to, scared of her
to this day. He knocks on every door, hoping for
somewhere to hide.

And?

        She always finds him.

You're missing the best part.

        Right. If you listen closely, you can hear her
breath rattling as she passes the houses, catching
up to him.

He pauses, forcing a silence only their breathing fills, and they
stifle their breaths despite themselves.

        And the last thing you hear before she does—
she always does—is the stable boy's last ever—

AHHHHHHHH!

        *—Scream!*

Hey!

She slaps his arm.

        You jumped.

You were scared.

You made me jump.

        Yeah,

He sniggers.

Out of your *skin*.

## SKELFREY WOODS

This is far enough, the woman says.

Are you sure? Her partner reads the map over her shoulder. Not holding it upside down again, are you?

She ignores the comment. Sure as I can be with "in Skelfrey Woods" to go on. She folds the map up again.

I thought there'd be something here, he says.

Like what?

I don't know. A sign. HERE LIES PEG FYFE—

*Quiet*, she hisses.

—WITCH OF WICSTUN! He nudges her side, jovial. No one's out here.

I don't fancy being on the receiving end of a shotgun, she says. We're trespassing. And anyway, she was hanged 300 years ago—*allegedly*. If you're looking for a blue plaque, that's it.

She points to a tree stump.

Well, he says. It'll have to do. He takes a picture of the stump and turns to her. I wonder if she's watching us. He pulls a face of mock terror.

The woman rolls her eyes. She feels as if they're being watched, but then she has felt that way since they passed the PRIVATE PROPERTY sign bordering the woods.

Peggy? She whispers, indulging him. Do you have a spoon we can borrow?

He snorts, setting her off too, and her unease dissipates.

A rustling silences them. They crouch low, covering their mouths.

What was that? He mouths.

She shakes her head, conscious that the daylight has faded in the past hour; that they're alone among the trees. The woods feel eerie without their chatter and with his wide eyes, all joking gone from them now. She could easily mistake the wind rattling the branches for a strangled breath in the silence.

He swears, exhaling beside her ear.

What? She pictures a shotgun barrel angled towards them, an apparition emerging amidst the trees, and grabs his arm.

Look, he says. She follows his gaze. It's a fucking rabbit.

The rabbit's nose twitches as it regards them, frozen among the leaves. She releases her breath.

Fucking rabbit, he repeats.

They start to laugh again, shakily.

We should get back, she says. Before it gets dark.

He doesn't argue this time.

When they turn back down the hill, her heart is still thumping. Head prickling as if more than a rabbit's eyes are following her.

## PEG

I like their fear. I always thought it was something that I could smell on the air, like blood, metallic and tangy.

I breathe it in, tasting every fearful whisper of my name.

I like their superstition, too. Their speculation. They have always been superstitious in this village. Crying "witchcraft" after every wicked deed and weaving intricacies into my life they still weave today. So shrouded in stories I've almost become one.

I want to tell them: there are worse evils than witches. Truths crueller than their fictions.

And the spoon?

It was wooden.

# ADAM HASSAN
# OCTOBER

Dirges, ditch
Culprits, a hitch
dark dank age
hunters, rage

poltergeists of Windle
red rock steps
beacons to
a Hamlett

At Crank Caverns
the timeslip's sleeve
loosens, upturned
on Hallow's Eve

An altar where impish fiends
chew the cadavers of the local cuisine
Robbers are led through shadowy chambers
Where the Hangman always labours

# ADAM HASSAN
# THE TWITCHER

I repeat my sentence and count on my legs
tapping my gut and cancerous eggs,
till they split on the floor
and silence the bark
of brain stew dribbling in the dark

Demons peer from puddles of the Apocalypse
Fangs of a Jackal at my neck
Nefarious cockroaches on the lino they skid
coating excrement on lackies of the tinfoil lid

vultures harness conspiracies
a cabal in cahoots,
then gnaw at the morsels
of bountiful loot

# C. J. SUBKO
# INCORRUPTIBLE

When the nun Sister Rosa died of tuberculosis, nobody was more surprised than Sister Rosa herself that her corpse failed to decay. She was not especially holy, nor rich, nor consequential—in short, not the kind of person over whom penitents would sit vigil for days and days until a stink should be detected. The kind of person who might be discovered Incorruptible.

For this reason, Sister Rosa was lucky, in some sense of the word, that she expired just a day before the abbey was bombed by the Americans, leaving no one alive to give her a proper burial—a burial that would have, in all likelihood, confined her miracle away from mortal eyes forever. But Sister Rosa, lying awake inside of the shell of her body, was wedged between two broken columns beneath a ceiling so cracked that the stars spilled inside.

For two years, she watched the progress of these stars. Watched as bombs blew across the sky, splashing it with red. Watched as fighter planes from the north dropped paratroopers into the countryside to fight.

To liberate.

And she prayed, and prayed, and prayed.

She prayed to God for comfort, in her darkness and her loneliness. In the sameness of her days.

It was not until a hot day in 1945 that Rosa heard footsteps. Not the padding of rabbits or the clip clop of deer, but human boots scuffing against the rubble.

"Aldo, Aldo!" cried a man's voice. "I think someone's alive over here."

## INCORRUPTIBLE

"Alive? Living here in the ruins?" The man snorted. "Marco, you pazzo, who would live up here."

"Just come, I think—oh."

Then he came upon her and he saw her, truly saw her. The waxy white skin polished and pure, stretching perfectly over her bones. The glassy brown eyes. The chapped lips, just a touch of blood pinking them, and the same two spots of liveliness in her cheeks.

A doll.

Marco fell to his knees and began making the sign of the cross. "Incorruptible."

Aldo sniggered, calling him a puta, but then he saw Sister Rosa too, one perfect body preserved among all the stinking, festering, skeletal corpses of the abbey. He too began making the sign of the cross, and he and Marco prayed together breathlessly for several minutes. Sister Rosa luxuriated in the sound of the Word, but more so, in any words, for she had been lonely, so lonely, simply staring up longingly at the stars, worried that the Lord had abandoned her by trapping her soul in this earthly prison.

But as she tried to cry out, she could not.

She was still dead.

Only now, she was discovered.

She prayed to Jesus his son, for serenity, as they took her. What would they do to her? What was life for a beautiful corpse?

†

Sister Rosa's body was interred in a grand glass coffin in the Basilica della Fiore del Dio, a beautiful coffin gilded at the joints with a glass lid for offerings and many, many flowers.

And she received both. Now that the war was over, many penitents came to praise God for its end, to ask for blessings to find missing family members, and to pray for help with their renewed lives.

And while they prayed, Sister Rosa prayed. She felt for them, these supplicants, and lying on her side, turned towards their faces, all she could see was their pain and their grief. Their fingerprints stained her glass, and the prints of their lips as they kissed her coffin.

The people came to see her in droves. Even il Papa came to see her, and he prayed to her not in Latin but in his native Polish. *Kochanie,* he called her. *Dear. Cud,* he called her. *Miracle.*

But the church would close at night, the lights off except for the candles, leaving Sister Rosa alone in the dark. She continued to pray, and pray, and pray. This time she prayed to her Mother Mary, for companionship. For who else could understand the loneliness of a woman who, in gaining immortality, had lost everything?

†

The years passed, and Sister Rosa remained in her coffin in the Basilica.

But the world around the Basilica was changing.

Penitents did not come to bring her flowers and to kiss her altar. Instead, idle, wayward tourists came once or twice a day with their five euros to snap flashing photographs of her waxy visage, to "ooh and ahh" and make faces.

And the janitors at closing time…some took the kind of liberties she could not bear to recall.

But worst still were the nights, these dark nights lit now only by battery powered candles. When Sister Rosa cried tears of perfumed oil that no one would see. When she prayed.

And prayed.

And prayed.

But this time, she did not pray for the penitents.

She did not pray for comfort, or serenity, or companionship.

This time, she prayed for oblivion.

# LINDA BROMILOW
# ALCHEMICAL

## MONDAY

"Shut that," Ben mumbled, hunching just that little bit further over the steering wheel, "it's bloody...irritating." He waved his hand in front of his face; it made a slapping sound as he plonked it back onto the wheel.

Rhia reluctantly pressed the button that had moments earlier promised fresh air and slumped a little in her seat as she listened to the slow electric whir of the passenger window, sucking back into its tight seal.

A trickle of sweat slid down her cleavage, pooling with the other droplets that had gathered, soaking her bra.

It had been Ben's idea to take a long summer break in the Welsh countryside, away from the sweltering, claustrophobia of the city; to escape the suffocating glass high-rises that bounce the suns scorching rays onto every exposed metal surface, transforming London into an open foundry.

Rhia watched the sunlight bounce off the car bonnet and Ben's blonde, blonde hair. She had once loved the contrast between his hair and her long black waves. Had loved the way his hair appeared to be glowing in summer, as if he was some ethereal being. She closed her eyes against the artificial brightness.

"That's the community centre slash pub. Only place you can get internet access," he blurted.

She jumped slightly in her seat and opened her eyes to Ben waving a hand in the general direction of a large, single-storey modern building. Just next to it was a road sign: 'Croeso Alcemegol. Population 513'

"We're here then," Rhia stated.

The car followed the dusty lane as it undulated and weaved its way between green fields. Rhia spotted the occasional track splintering off; some dotted with houses, some seemingly leading to nowhere. Ben turned the car down one of these narrow inlets, where a squat thatched cottage sat in a dead-end. He turned the engine off and cranked the handbrake. Rhia began to survey the surroundings. There was no way out.

Must've took a wrong turn, she thought.

Ben released his seat belt, grinned at Rhia and got out of the car, slamming the door shut. Rhia closed her eyes to the welcome gust of air and imagined the door slamming over and over. Eventually, she peered through the dusty windscreen at the cottage. A scrubby patch of sun-scorched grass, divided by a barely visible path, which led to a substantial, ancient wooden door; a door that somehow seemed more akin to a castle than a cottage. Either side of the door were filthy windows, deep-set in a fading yellow frontage. A small, cracked wooden sign hung next to the door: 'Yew Cottage'.

Rhia turned in her seat and looked back toward the lane. On the opposite side was a lush field, fenced and populated with sheep. She locked eyes with one of its inhabitants as it chewed the cud. A thrum crept into her mind, low, deep and steady; it seeped and fanned out in her chest. Ben came into view and opened the car boot. Rhia coughed and turned back to the front of the car, fumbling in her bag in the foot well for the now tepid bottle of water.

"Come on." Ben headed down the grassy path with their suitcases. Rhia reluctantly got out of the car.

"This isn't the place you showed me on the internet," she called after him.

"This is better," he shot back over his shoulder and disappeared into the darkness beyond the door.

"Cheaper. Cheaper is what you mean," Rhia muttered. The threshold was deep, so much so she had to grab the doorframe to stop from falling into the entrance hall. A slow, sharp pain stabbed at the centre of her left palm and radiated up her arm.

"Shit!" She inspected her hand. The tip of a fat, dark splinter was flush with the waxy, red flesh of her palm. She pulled back her fingers, hoping the splinter would poke out enough to remove it: it stayed put.

"Ben," she shouted and headed through the door at the back of the entrance hall. It led to an open-plan kitchen living area, flooded with light through a wall of glass doors. It definitely wasn't what she expected from the exterior.

She made her way across the slate floor, lifted the door handle and pushed. The doors glided, each one folding gently onto the next until the whole of the room was open to the elements. The verdant vista that greeted her had everything she could have wished for: a mature cottage garden with swaying, grand evergreens bordering to the right opening out onto not-too-distant hills that gradually petered out to the left, toward sea-cliffs. Maybe she could be happy here.

## TUESDAY

The bedroom was stifling and Rhia spent most of the night staring at the ceiling. She rose early, showered, put on a black cotton summer dress and went down to the kitchen where Ben was draining a glass of orange juice.

"I'm going to walk into the village for some supplies," she said. "Fancy joining me?"

She watched him grab his car keys and laptop from the coffee table.

"Can't. Need to finish up some work on the project. I'm off to the community centre."

"Work? We're on holiday." Rhia looked at him imploringly.

"We're here for weeks, we've got loads of time to explore." He left.

Rhia dropped a bottle of cold water into her cloth bag and headed out the front door, determined to have herself a gorgeous day. In the field of sheep by the lane was a man, busying himself around a scarecrow.

Rhia noticed they both wore the same dog-eared tweed suit. As the man began to top it all off with a flat cap, she caught a glimpse of the scarecrow's face: large blue eyes, straight nose and full lips, all framed by glossy, black curly hair. The eyes blinked and a knowing smile spread across its lips. Can't be – she shook her head and walked away, but the same thrum from the day before began to fill her mind. She listed, her tongue stuck to the roof of her mouth and her skin became clammy. She stumbled to the roadside and found a rock large enough to sit on. The plastic bottle crackled and collapsed slightly as she rapidly drank some water. She hitched her dress up mid-thigh and pressed her bare skin against the rock, the surface cooling her blood as it circulated and married up with the refreshing water in her stomach and throat. She closed her eyes, relishing the pleasure as she shifted her weight from one leg to the other.

"Are you alright dear?" A reedy voice broke the spell. She opened her eyes. A small, silver haired, elderly woman in a 1970's housecoat and brown slippers, hunched inches from Rhia's face.

"O! O, I'm fine, thank you." She quickly grabbed her bag and continued her journey.

The lane widened where the village shop sat in the middle of a terraced row. It was the widest of the seven houses, with a large, half-frosted window painted with blue lettering declaring the owner to be D M Mellors. Cracked, white paving stones marked out its boundary with the lane. The bell that heralded her entrance was the old-fashioned manual type, rocking back and forth each time the door hit it.

"Good morning." Rhia nodded and smiled at the grey-haired man who greeted her. She liked his rosy cheeks and the gentle rhythmic way he continued to stock the shelves as she made her way in. A quick glance at her surroundings was enough to know there hadn't been a refit since the late 60's but they had the basics. She gathered what she needed and placed the items on the Formica counter. The shopkeeper began to calmly ring everything through the archaic till. The punching of the keys and the clunk and whir of the receipt roll were hypnotic.

"On holiday?" he asked.

"Yes, we're here 'til September. A bit of 'R and R'." As she spoke the words her shoulders relaxed and her eyes half-closed.

"Staying up at the barn?"

Rhia dreamily shook her head. "No. No, at Yew cottage."

"Maaarge!" he shouted.

She was snapped out of her reverie. The shopkeeper froze, box of eggs in hand, staring at Rhia, his eyes sparkling with excitement.

"Maaarge!" he bellowed again. "My wife," he explained with a smile.

The colourful nylon ribbons hanging in the doorway behind him rustled and a short, dark haired, middle-aged lady appeared. Rhia noted the perm, the large glasses and the pink cotton dress: all straight out of the 80's.

"Dai?" Marge looked at Rhia.

"This lady is staying at Yew Cottage." He slowly gestured in wonder toward Rhia. Marge peered over her glasses, nodded, pointed upwards and disappeared back through the nylon ribbons.

"She'll be back." Dai pulsed his shoulders twice and smiled.

"Welcome." Marge warmly greeted Rhia on her return and pressed something into her left hand. Rhia winced as the rough, warm object scratched at the splinter in her palm.

"O, I am sorry dear." Marge, with delicate concern, opened Rhia's hand.

"It's ok," said Rhia, "I just have a splinter from the cottage door. That's what the witch hazel is for." She gestured to her shopping. Dai surreptitiously moved the bottle of liquid under the counter.

"Yew, my love." Marge nodded and curled Rhia's fingers firmly around the object. "All will be well."
A soothing coolness seemed to bathe the wound.

"Your shopping," Dai said, and placed the laden bag over Rhia's right shoulder.

"Thank you," she smiled.

Marge gently pulled Rhia toward her, an intensity about her face and shoulders, and whispered, "Are you wood or stone?"

Rhia prised her hand from Marge's grasp. "Um, I, er, thanks for the shopping."

She jerked open the door and darted from the shop, the bell ringing double-time. She inspected Marge's gift on the walk back to Yew Cottage. A rough piece of dark tree bark, no more than three inches long, and a smooth, grey stone, similar in size. They had been tied together with a short length of jute twine. Rhia hadn't noticed how intently she had been studying the object until she reached the cottage door, sticky and with a raging thirst. She jammed the key into the lock. The thrum bellowed in her ears and throbbed in her chest; she was pushed to her knees by the weight of it. As she grabbed the door handle and strained to pull herself to her feet, a pair of thick, heavy arms encircled her torso and tightened. She looked down and saw the same, dog-eared tweed from earlier that morning. A scream sat in her throat, suppressed, pressing and expanding. Heat from someone exhaling rushed by her ear swirling with the words, "Are you wood or stone?"

Her scream was released: guttural and raw. She spun round, wildly throwing punches and slaps into thin air. Exhausted and crying she willed herself to look toward the field: a flat cap sat atop a wooden cruciform.

## THURSDAY

Rhia was upstairs in the bathroom when she heard Ben return from the community centre. He'd spent the last couple of days there working on 'the project', while Rhia had pottered around the cottage, reading and baking. Thursday afternoon had been passed lying on the tiled bathroom floor wearing only her knickers and bra. She was listening to Ben move about the kitchen when a shrill noise in the garden caught her attention. Standing on the closed toilet seat, she pushed the window open to its full extent in order to get a better view.

The silver haired woman in the 70's housecoat and brown slippers was wandering around the garden.

Rhia initially thought she was randomly wandering around, chunnering to herself, but she soon noticed a pattern. The woman would touch a tree with her left hand mutter something, walk to a stone bench on the opposite side of the garden, place her left hand on it and mutter again, walk to the centre of the garden with both hands aloft, let out a small shriek to the hills, to the sea and finally to the cottage.

She shouted down to Ben, "There's some old bat in the garden!"

"What's she holding?" she said to herself. There was something writhing in the woman's right hand, pulsing as if it were trying to break free.

"She's got a bird." Rhia turned from the window and shouted, "She's got a bird!"

The woman faced the cottage, kissed the bird and released it. A sudden rush of air forced Rhia from the toilet to the floor, birdsong and a cacophony of beating wings filled the room.

"What're you doing down there?" Ben stood over her, hands in his trouser pockets.

She pushed herself onto her haunches and hugged her knees. "There was an old woman in the garden with a bird. No, she had loads of birds."

Ben stood on his tiptoes and glanced out of the bathroom window. "Well, there's no one there." He looked at her and raised his eyebrows as he walked to the door. "I think this heat is getting to you."


**FRIDAY**

Rhia accompanied Ben to the community centre, despite his protestations. She didn't want to spend another day of the holiday stuck in the cottage while he spent at least eight hours tied to his laptop. When lunchtime approached, Rhia asked if he would stop for the day and maybe go for a drive.

"One wage earner in the family means that person has to work twice as hard to pay for holidays, the home, the car." He typed furiously then sat back in his chair; arms folded. "Though, we're still not a family, are we?" He glanced her way, stony faced, then continued to type.

Rhia tried to bare the silence. She closed her eyes, pressed her lips together and pushed them between her teeth. "I think I'll have a mooch."

In a small back room, she found an exhibition of photos and art prints. A black and white photo drew her particular attention; it was of a standing stone out of which protruded two human arms, palms outstretched as if in rapt glory. She moved in close to study it. How was the trick turned?

"Claud Cahun." It was Marge. "Great photo. Wonderful little illusion. Have you seen these over here?"

Marge directed Rhia to the opposite side of the room. "Ithell Colquhoun. Not original, of course, these are prints of her work. She had such a marvellous way, interpreting nature and the body. This one is her in the bath."

Rhia recognised the two rocky outcrops protruding from the sea as thighs, a piece of brown seaweed floating between them. She moved to the last picture and remarked that it was very different from the others.

"This is Ernst, not Colquhoun. The Robing of the Bride."

Rhia studied the picture. The bride being readied for the ceremony, naked save for a red robe and a splendid owl headdress, one cool, blue eye looking out from behind the mask. A strange bird-like creature stood by her side holding a broken spear, and by her feet, a four-teeted green goblin, pregnant, a red robe draped over its head. She turned to ask Marge more about it, but she had left.

Rhia tried to row the small, wooden boat between two large rocky outcrops, but the seaweed wrapped around the oars, forcing her to jump overboard and swim ashore. Halfway up the beach, Ben was on all fours thrusting his groin at nothing. She pushed him over onto his back, revealing a VR headset strapped across his eyes. She kicked him and ran from the beach to the field of sheep. The scarecrow was lashed to his cruciform, naked save for an owl mask, his skin the rough bark of a yew tree. She stared at the cool, blue eye behind the mask and told him she would be both.

## SATURDAY

Rhia woke with a jump, almost rolling off the sofa, and was immediately aware of a burning sensation in her left hand. She was gripping the stone and bark, now sticky with the red, resinous substance oozing from the splinter; she let it fall to the floor. The cottage door slammed: Ben had left for the community centre. She raised her arms and held her hands out in protestation, then let them flop on her stomach.

"Of course he's gone to the sodding community centre. Some sodding holiday this is."

She prised herself off the sofa and stomped upstairs to the bathroom.

"Scarecrows, old bats, birds, sodding bloody wood and sodding stone!" She splashed her face with cold water and quickly soaped and rinsed her armpits.

"I think this heat is getting to you," she echoed Ben's words mockingly to herself in the mirror.

"Maybe it is," she looked up at the bathroom window, her hands against the cold porcelain of the sink.

She resolved to get out, explore the village more. She recalled reading something about a local church. She rifled through some drawers and finally landed on a pamphlet on the console table in the entrance hall.

"St. Catherine's." She flipped the leaflet over where there was a map of its location and opening times.

She passed through the lychgate, which headed a path to the church. Two enormous, ancient yew trees stood sentinel either side of the path. Rhia stopped to admire their solemn splendour, running her right hand across the coarse, warm bark. From the other side of the tree she heard scrabbling and rustling, as if something were searching amongst a pile of dead leaves. She stealthily tiptoed toward the noise; her breath and muscles held tight in anticipation.

There was a sharp, animalistic screech as something hurtled toward her, forcing her back against the tree. The screech came again, this time from a static position: the church porch. On the little wooden roof sat a Barn Owl, seemingly scrutinising Rhia as its head bobbed rhythmically. She still wanted to see inside, so hunched and ran through the porch, entering the back half of the church. Inside, the church was cool and dark. Heady incense smoke coiled from a thurible hanging on a tall, brass stand.

"Catholic," she whispered and leant back against the closed door, gazing at the serpent of smoke as it wound its way through the feint sunlight, mingling with the dancing dust motes as they sparkled, sprite-like.

"Hello?" A well-spoken male voice carried around the church. Her heart sank at the realisation she didn't have the place to herself.

"Hello?" The voice came again.

Rhia pigeon walked to the end of the aisle. A tall, thin priest bobbed into view. Middle-aged and strawberry blonde, the floor-length black cassock he wore gave him the appearance of having been stretched.

"Welcome. Welcome to St. Catherine's." He held his hands out to Rhia then clasped them to his chest as if in prayer. Rhia gave him a little wave. He took this to be an invitation and immediately began chatting about the history of the church in an enthusiastic stream of consciousness, his body in an elegant perpetual motion, guiding her to mark certain interesting features.

"Are you a churchgoer yourself?" he finally asked, coming to rest by the altar.

"No." She shook her head and looked guiltily to the floor. She'd always disliked that about herself: the grain of shame that lurked in her stomach whenever some ecclesiastic questioned her faith, or lack of it.

"No," he shook his head and looked mournfully about the church, as if it might be the final time he would see its beauty. "Not many attend these days. We get ten, maybe twelve, on a Sunday. The crowds tend to arrive midsummer," he looked to the stained-glass window beyond the altar, "but not for the big man."

He shot her a resigned smile. "I'm the third incumbent here in eighteen months. The chap before me took off with all the valuables, portable property, and his predecessor went mad, ringing the bells at all hours."

He gave a weak laugh then fell silent, staring at the floor. Rhia decided to steer the conversation away from mad priests by asking about the green men and ouroboros symbols dotted about the church.

"Ah, yes: to appease the pagans. Bit creepy aren't they?" he said, wiggling his fingers mid-air. She was about to say she found them fascinating when he pointed to a small, shadowy alcove to the right of the altar.

"We have a relic. That didn't get pinched. Come. Look." He beckoned her over to the gloomy corner.

On a small, oak table was a domed, glass case. Housed within the case was a solitary, metal finger; engraved and standing erect. In the centre of the finger a small rectangle of metal had been cut away, making a window of sorts, through which mummified flesh could be seen. Rhia leaned in to get a closer look. The priest mirrored her, his rough cassock brushed against her bare ankle. He began to speak in a low, reverent whisper, "St. Catherine of Alexandria. Sentenced to death on a breaking wheel when she refused to renounce God. She shattered the wheel with one touch." He glanced at Rhia, then back at the finger.

"They cut off her head and, instead of blood, a milky fluid poured from the wound. Amongst a litany of peoples claiming her, she's the patron saint of maidens."

Rhia felt the priest's cassock shift and settle against her calf.

"Are you a maiden?" He slowly turned to her.

"Well, I'd better be off!" Rhia quickly cleared the length of the church.

"Wouldn't you like to touch it?" she heard the priest shout as she made the churchyard. She leant on one of the yew trees to catch her breath, keeping one eye on the church.

"Are you alright dear?" Rhia recognised the reedy voice of the silver haired woman in the 70's housecoat and brown slippers. She made to leave, but the woman gripped Rhia's wrist.

"You're not to go yet," she said, "this bleeding tree requests your presence." She led Rhia round the other side of the tree where, around chest height on the trunk, a blood-like substance seeped from a stump, as if a limb had recently been amputated.

"Ah, the bleeding yew," Rhia said. "The Priest was just telling me the church sees this as a representation of the blood of Christ."

"Pah!" spat the woman. "These trees are older than the church. That's no more Christ's blood than I'm John the flippin' Baptist."

Rhia laughed a little and began to feel at ease with the woman.

"There's something older than that fairy-tale." She jabbed a finger in the direction of the church then crouched at the base of the tree and plunged her fingers into the dark soil, releasing a rich, earthy scent.

"Something deep in the earth."

The thrum began pulsing in time with the movement of the old woman's fingers as they dug and sank deeper.
Rhia heard a deep intake of breath at the nape of her neck, then a hot whisper asked, "Are you wood or are you stone? Or are you both?"

She stumbled forward and fell against the tree, unable to speak. Without a word and with great ease, the old woman lifted Rhia to her feet and led her to a clearing at the side of the church, where there was a small ring of standing stones. Some had fallen and lay flat, whilst others leaned tiredly against their neighbours. At the centre of the circle was a prehistoric passage tomb, covered with grass and pink Windflowers, its two stone entrances tall enough to admit an adult.

The woman sat Rhia on one of the prostrate slabs.

"That's the third time this week," Rhia slurred.

The woman pressed her hands against Rhia's abdomen; her papery, liver-spotted skin belied the strength emitted by her bony fingers.

"Quickening!" With rapid eye movements, she appeared to be searching Rhia's face for something.

"Impossible," Rhia mumbled, as she lay back against the cool, cool stone.

## SUNDAY

Rhia's eyelids fluttered as the morning light beckoned her to wake. Between soft, slow blinks, she caught glimpses of a small flock of birds taking flight. She watched them dance and cut silently through the sky before realising she was outdoors. Where she lay was uncomfortable and there was something hard and fat digging into the base of her spine. She pushed up onto her knees and looked back to where she had lain. Glossy, damp grass flattened into a swirling circle pattern, at the centre of which sat a rotten stump of wood, poking out of the claggy soil. She stood, her saturated dress clinging to the back of her legs, and looked across the rest of the field. It was dry and patchy. Tired, she climbed the fence and trudged to the cottage.

"Where've you been? I've been so worried." Ben paced up and down the kitchen. "It's been chaos. The river surged and almost burst its banks. The priest was drowned in his car. Suitcases and bibles all over the place."

"The river?" Rhia asked, confused.

"Yeees. The river." Ben tutted and looked at her as if she were an imbecile. "They reckon it was some freak overflow from the hills." He stopped pacing and looked out into the garden. "Yeah, so. The project calls." he said, picking up his laptop from the kitchen worktop, waggling it as he left the cottage.

Incredulity momentarily rooted Rhia to the spot. In stunned silence, she slid her shoes from her feet and walked barefoot to the glass doors, the slate floor easing and cooling her hot, aching feet with each step. As she absently stared out into the garden, monstrous, black storm clouds steadily filled the sky, barring the sunlight, creating the illusion of night-time's arrival. There was a tremendous low-slung roll of thunder and a silent flash of lightning.

Rhia thought she saw the scarecrow in the illumination.

"I'm going mad." She closed her eyes and counted to ten. When she opened them, the silver haired woman was standing in front of her.

"Jesus!" Rhia fell backwards onto the floor.

The old woman proffered up a dead, white goose. Its fat, limp body lay across her arms, the head flopped to one side with its bill open revealing the saw-like tomia and pink muscular tongue, the piercing blue, dead eye stared at Rhia. Its throat had been cut and viscous, dark blood dripped to the floor. The woman's eyes were milky white and her jaw slack, her tongue writhing in the dark cavern of her mouth. She began walking, trance-like, toward Rhia, slipping slightly on the blood. Rhia's left hand began to throb. The resinous red substance began to leak from the splinter wound and the thrum, louder than ever, filled the room – it was coming from the old woman's gaping maw. Rhia tried to cry out, but her throat contracted, she couldn't breathe.

The thrum stopped as if it had sucked itself down into the old woman's throat and dragged all the air from the room with it. Her jaw snapped shut and the goose spontaneously combusted. Rhia rapidly shuffled back into a corner and instinctively wrapped her arms about her head. A deafening, guttural primeval wail rushed towards her.

"Rhia!" A hand gripped her wrist. "Rhia! I heard screaming and saw smoke."

Rhia recognised Marge's voice and opened her eyes.

"Your grill was on fire love." She beckoned with both hands for Rhia to stand.

"The grill? What? No?" Rhia looked around the smoke-filled room as Marge walked her to the sofa and sat her down.

"No, no. The old woman was here," she said, firmly pointing to the middle of the room, "and she had a dead goose. She had a dead goose and it burst into flames."

Marge softly sat beside Rhia and gently placed a hand on her thigh.

"The goose of Hermes Trismegistus." She smiled.

Rhia frowned at her.

"You're nearly there my love."

"Where?" Rhia asked as she complied with the rhythmic movements of Marge laying her down.

"You'll embrace it. A half-life is no life at all. Now rest, you'll need all your strength for tomorrow."

"What do I do tomorrow?" she asked, drifting to sleep. "You'll know my love, you'll know."


## MONDAY

Rhia woke to the noise of the kettle boiling and Ben banging cupboard doors.

"Oh, you're awake then." He splashed milk into a mug and onto the kitchen worktop. He tutted and muttered, "Fuck's sake." He attempted to mop up the mess with kitchen roll.

"It's rammed out there." He waved his hand in the direction of the lane as if shooing something away.

Rhia inspected her hand. There was a hard, amber blob encasing the embedded splinter. She tapped it. There was something satisfying about the tic, tic, ticking sound her nail and the golden dome created.

"Midsummer madness!" Ben said with derision. "I couldn't get onto the carpark at the community centre. So much for getting away from it all."

A couple of bangs on the front door were followed by a cheery, "Hello!"

Marge walked into the room wearing a black, gossamer dress. She gave a twirl and fluffed up the frills at her shoulders. "No, no, do come in." Ben sarcastically waved her in.

Rhia and Marge embraced. "You're ready," Marge whispered to her. She gently pushed Rhia back; held both of her hands and with a slight cock of her head, they both went upstairs.

"Don't mind me." Ben wobbled his head as he wiped the worktop.

Rhia loved the way her dress trailed behind her as she walked down the stairs. The drag and pull of the soft, red cotton against her chest made her feel taller.

For a moment, Ben felt his lungs expanding, as if some heavy obstruction had dissolved from the centre of his chest as he watched Rhia twirl, fanning out the skirts of her dress in rhythmic undulations. His throat tightened; he'd always disliked her wearing that red dress. As they danced out of the cottage, Rhia and Marge beckoned for Ben to follow them.

The lane was alive with a great parade of people dressed in colourful, flowing garments and ribbons. They danced with abandoned glory, following the drums, hurdy-gurdys, flutes and bagpipes. Every celebrant had flowers with them: midsummer poles, garlands, freezes, posies and bouquets – the perfume drifting on the air filled the whole village with the most glorious scent. Rose petals appeared to cascade from the sky, nestling in Rhia's hair.

The throng danced its way through the village. Dai joined as it snaked by his shop, whooping with joy.

"At last," he cried and span Rhia round, kissing her on both cheeks.

"Ben!" He embraced him. Ben's arms hung limply by his sides. "Be sure to make it all the way to the stones."

Dai placed a garland of Red Spider Lillies over Ben's head, shook his hand then danced away.

When they reached the churchyard, Rhia danced to the bleeding Yew and pressed her left hand against the stump. The resin was soft and warm as it enveloped her hand, pulling her into the concentric circles.

The parade became a half-remembered thing as every rasp and nick against her flesh were as kisses from a lover. Her hair tangled and writhed deep, nourished by water, mycelium and mulch. Her fingers and toes photosynthesised, swelling and deflating, pushing out purifying oxygen. Birds nestled in her breast, their tiny hearts fluttering, vibrating against her eardrums.

They made a gift of their delicate eggshells; each one crushed and absorbed onto her abdomen.

"Time to greet the stones," she heard Dai whisper.

She was alone. She could hear the melody of the parade carry from the stone circle. For a moment she stayed by the tree, relishing the cushiony moss beneath her feet: her shoes were gone.

The stone circle fell silent as Rhia approached. The parade had joined hands and encircled the outer edges twice over. Marge left the circle and approached her.

"You've torn your dress my love."

Rhia touched her right hip where a triangle of fabric was missing; her skin was wet with blood.

"Not to worry," Marge said, "easily mended." She threaded her fingers through Rhia's and pressed against her bloodied palm.

"Come."

They walked slowly to the passage tomb where Dai stood, barring the way to the entrance. He held a steel, two-edged sword with a copper and silver hilt, an ouroboros engraved on the pommel.

Two female voices began to sing in harmony, low and soft. Rhia didn't recognise the language, but understood the medieval lament.

Dai presented Rhia with the sword and she accepted, grasping the handle with both hands pointing the blade to the sky, the cool steel almost touching her face. Dai bowed deeply and stood aside, leaving the way open. No light penetrated the centre of the tomb, but Rhia sensed Ben's presence; the dark seemed more-so.

She deliberately dragged the sword across the stone roof, small sparks sprang from its tip.

"Who's there?" He was turning in panicked circles. "What's going on?"

She kissed the cold steel and whispered, "I am both."

# ALI MALONEY
# TWO SEVERED FINGERS IN THE RAMSGRAFT STIGMATA

You were told not to look.

Below, in the streets: the Shepherd drives his flock through the city.

Ornate glass facades opening onto banks and insurance firms are smeared with shit, mats of fur, and tortured bleats. Shutters come down. Curtains are drawn. The last few running feet disappear into subways and stairwells before the Shepherd comes past.

You can't resist looking.

It's not like you should be here anyway. You're the only one in the building today. As a lowly temp, five days a week in the office is mandatory for your "collaboration"... which is insane as you are normally the only one in.

You don't want to have to work but you need the money.

The conference room is dark. The lights went down automatically when the Shepherd came. The rest of your team are frozen in awkward dropped connection expressions on the huge screen across the far wall. The speaker phone crackles out a distorted loop of the last thing said. Something about a report you should have already finished but that you don't even know how to start. The admonishment echoes relentlessly. If they want you to do a good job, they should be better at guiding you, showing you what to do.

You don't want to work, so you're glad of the distraction.

ALI MALONEY
TWO SEVERED FINGERS IN THE RAMSGRAFT STIGMATA

It's hard to untangle the sight of knotted, stitched limbs and joints amongst the ebb of black encrusted wool and snapping snouts, tearing at cars, churning asphalt. Curls and coils could almost be tucked wings, bulging pustules as hooves. Gnarled horns unfurl upwards like marching banners. Reflections in the glass-fronted offices double the throng. The Shepherd is a centauric maelstrom in the centre. You can't distinguish his steed from the seethe. His fleece billowing and bells — grafted into his knuckles — toll as he cracks a barb-tipped black whip. The window pane shakes against your face. You didn't realise you had pressed up so close.

All the windows across from you are normally bustling with busy, productive workers in suits hurrying around. Now, they are all empty and black.

Who told you not to look? Why? This is just one crappy temp job in a series of crappy temp jobs. In the absence of any better plans or knowing what to do with your life, you've just sleep-walked through so many mind-numbing inductions and mandatory training and competency questionnaires that they all blur together. Maybe it came up in one of those. You long for someone to tell you what to do.

Behind, a whirr and screech startles you. The fax machine, long since reduced to nothing more than a stack of used coffee cups and misplaced PowerPoint print-outs, is summoning a page. The glue smeared display cannot render the sender's phone number. The characters, trailing ink blots, swirl into a dense smudge at the paper's centre, a rhapsody rendered in messy ASCII. It's nonsense and noise. You take the page and return to the window.

Below, in the streets: the Shepherd is looking up. He sees you. The flock is baying hungrily. A chorus of ferocious black eyes pour into the lobby, disappearing from sight, becoming a bleating rumble up the stairwell. The Shepherd is coming for you.

Is this why no one comes into the office anymore? Have they left you here as some sort of sacrifice? Could none of them take pity on you? Not even Janet, who smiles and brings you coffee? Wait, is that what the fax is? Some sort of archaic life-line that someone has thrown? Some sort of protective...thing?

The characters are too jumbled to make out. You can't read anything but can tell that there are words buried in there. You go to the whiteboard and start to transcribe the underlying text as best you can. Digging through the layers, characters, words, phrases, and symbols emerge. You recognise the letters of your own name repeated several times.

The ink runs red.

The words swim more than they did in the original.

The room spins. You stumble as the wall underneath the words becomes membranous.

You can hear the maaing grow closer and the sound of doors crumbling as the stench of their hellish farm clatters up the building. You don't have much time.

The tip of your pen dips through the fabric of the wall. The vortex of text bends inwards, pulsing, breathing. Somewhere, behind — far behind you now — you are aware of the door bursting inwards, the Shepherd, and his flock flooding the room. But you are beyond them.

You fall through.

✝

Across the bare stone floor of the cottage, your grandmother tends to the fireplace. As she feeds the fire, your grandmother gives a name to each of the sticks before putting them in. You recognise your own, hers, and those not with you anymore. From the pot hanging above, a thin stew that is little more substantial than tea smells of yarrow and nutmeg. The wood is wet and burns with spittle and hiss. There are no flames that can warm either of you. Not tonight.

"No, I've already told you," she turns to you, her eyes glistening. "You can't go out. Not during harvest."

# ALI MALONEY
## TWO SEVERED FINGERS IN THE RAMSGRAFT STIGMATA

"How do you know it is tonight?" you ask.

"Sometimes, you just know. Stay away from the windows."

"But harvesting what?" You think of the scorched, barren lands that surround the cottage in almost every direction.

"In so many ways, you are still a child. That is not how the land — or the harvest — works."

"Then tell me, please."

"It is best not to speak of the Shepherd or think of his flock. We just need to stay in, protect ourselves as best we can. Here, drink this."

Outside, the wind howls and the thatched roof bristles.

"Who is the Shepherd? Why has he come?"

"Without the harvest, we have nothing," your grandmother says.

"We already have nothing."

"Not for long." A sudden stench and howl pierce through you. "He takes away boys and girls who don't know what to do with themselves, lost when there's no cause to be." She studies you. "Even worse are those who know what they should be doing but don't have the wit to go about it. And in return…"

You look down at the illustration you wanted to start. Or maybe it's a woodcarving, or a piece of writing, or a hat to knit. You know best what it is you wish you could do.

"Now, child, make yourself useful. I need you here. If you were taken, well, I don't think I'd manage without you. Come, the window boards need repairing."

You know better than to protest but you're no good at manual work. The hammer and nails are clumsy in your hands. You manage to hit the only nail once before missing and smashing the plank that keeps the window shut. You're not sure if the sound is the glass breaking or your grandmother screaming, but you can't help but look outside.

It is dark, despite the hour. As you look, trying to discern any shapes or familiar landmarks — the dead apple tree should be just outside — the darkness moves. It is a wall of black pelt, pushed up against the cottage. Stubby, bulging limbs and eyes poke through splitting wounds, searching for you. A warm wheezing breath — a confusing mixture of predatorial grunts and aroused sighs — washes over you. It is intoxicating and nauseous. Your grandmother pushes you roughly out the way.

"The compass and harness! Quick!"

You stumble towards the fire to grab her things. In your frantic dash, you knock the pot over, spilling it everywhere and dousing the small and feeble flames. A brutal chill instantly fills the room.

Your grandmother mutters something and dunks her hand into the small burlap pouch of salt that hangs from her girdle. She smashes the compass, bends its needle, and straps it to her two salt-encrusted forefingers. One of the beast's injuries is suckling through the broken window like a red, hungry, salivating mouth. Your grandmother thrusts her work deep into the gash.

"Be lost from these walls, this place, these lands. Shadow of disaster, go from this earth! Know no way!" Knuckles, tendons, and muscle tearing, she snaps her fingers completely off. Her scream gives her voice the last of her strength, "go beneath the earth or fly to the skies but this house is not your path!"

She collapses, bleeding, crying, and panting.

Frost and darkness overwhelm the house. You can not hear or see anything apart from your own anxious breath. Feeling your way across the stone floor, reaching for where your grandmother was, you fall and do not stop falling.

The shore is littered with bodies.

## ALI MALONEY
## TWO SEVERED FINGERS IN THE RAMSGRAFT STIGMATA

You step from the decaying rowboat onto the rocky beach. In front of you, encircled by five standing stones, the Shepherd stands, singing, beckoning you.

You should go to him.

There's not really any other choice.

Sorry. You can't put it off any longer.

You pick your way over the shingle and rough gravel. Remnants of your paperwork and the cottage floor are buried under shards of bones and shell, scratching at your bare feet. The wind whips dust from inside corpses — both human and animal — as if it were spores. Torn strips of faces are stretched out across the beach. Despite their mutilation, you recognise moments from their features, if not the people who might have worn them.

That's it. Keep going.

Not long now.

An elongated moustache, nailed to the ground with rusted pins, sparks thoughts of your belligerent bully of a boss. It is a shitty job with no prospects for promotion, or fulfilment. But what else could you possibly do? What skills do you have? Do you even know what it is you'd be happy doing?

A small shrubbery of tattooed arms and legs sprout as you walk past. The designs are too faded and moiled with scars to resemble anyone you remember, but still memories come. Lost loves, missed chances, misspoken arguments, and clumsy exploits; it's downright embarrassing how clueless you have gone about so many of these. Did you at least learn something about what makes you happy?

No? That's OK. You're almost there.

Don't stop.

Even without prompting, let the echoes of your life flood you. That's it. It's the only way now. Your last argument with your father. That time you passed someone in distress and didn't stop to help. Every time you put others before yourself, without any understanding of what they wanted. What would you have done differently?

You're almost ready.

Keep going.

You approach the circle of stones around the Shepherd. They are not stones at all. They are tangled, squashed sculpts of carcasses, their greying, flabby skin squeezed into monoliths. Antlers pierce skin. Nerve twitches flit as ripples across twisted limbs and hide. Puckered, oozing holes and mouths are red pockmarked keyholes in the pillars. The Shepherd sings to you.

"What do you want?" you might ask, or maybe "please help me." Or, perhaps, "do you have some water?" It doesn't matter. It's time.

These bodies have purpose.

You probably don't know what to do.

Step to the nearest pillar. See, there is a gap. You'd fit in so perfectly. There's no need to be afraid. You will never again know worry or doubt. You'll never want for anything. The other bodies shift, moaning and bleating softly, as you climb onto them. They take you into themselves. It is warm. Peaceful, isn't it? You're doing the right thing; the honourable thing, you know.

The harvest is you.

And they will know what you have done for them. It's really the best you could have hoped to do with your life.

The harvest is you. The yield will be magnificent.

# LAURA CATHCART
# THOMASIN

On her knees, absent of mind and resolute to her fate, she remained immune to the remedies of the local healer. A horseshoe hung above the threshold, the oil from the Jasmine bloom smeared across her soft stomach, the once beloved feline cast from their abode, did nothing to deter the curses that smothered them.

He was desperate and all consumed - he could not contain this any longer.

He heard rumouring of an unknown traveller, clad in blood red, who had sat for three days and three nights beneath the Rowan. His trepidation prolonged the encounter but by the next night, he decided he could watch his Love suffer no more, and went out to seek the counsel of this stranger.

As the sun began its descent behind the formidable hills above, the Stranger listened intently to him as stories of the plague on their household tumbled from his lips. He recounted the assumed curse that had fallen on her; how she spent the darkest hours wailing as a mother who had lost her firstborn. The days she spent unmoving in the corner of the darkened room, hands fixed and eyes glazed – how it seemed her head was awash with a procession of daemons and witches, that scoured for their next residence.

After this fraught monologue, the Stranger, resolute in her words, weaved tales of similarly afflicted and the curses that have bestowed themselves upon other households. She shared secrets and remedies of those long passed who had managed to break free. Milk baths and rotten fruit. Bitter yet clarifying herbal mixtures, pressed into sliced flesh as incantations were muttered; painful yes, but no more so than the toothache that currently besieged them.

"Their Devils will disappear to another place and you will be free of their burden, the Stranger claimed. This ritual must be carried out when evil appears to her, or in the light of the full moon."

He desperately agreed and the Stranger advised him to retrieve a glass vial, cleansed with birch smoke;

> Blood drawn from the current cycle
> Nails, thorns, hair
> Glass, wine, and wood
> Bone, salt, sugar.
> Sage, knotted threads and coins.
> Buried at the furthest corner of the house or
> Beneath the hearth or
> Concealed in walls – or inscribed on wooden posts
>
> The bottle will snare the evil
> Entangle it in the hair and knotted thread
> Impale it on nails, thorns, glass
> Drown it in the blood and the wine
> Hair, bone and wood will absorb
>
> She will be scrubbed clean with the salt, sugar and sage.

That night the full moon hung as an unblinking eye, its pale light casting jagged shadows through the slats of the shuttered casement. He followed the Stranger's instructions to the letter, gathering each required item with a trembling hand, whispering lamentations to the feline cast out, to the home that had withstood so much. The vial, blackened with wisps of birch smoke, was placed on the wooden table at the center of their dwelling.

As he carried out the aforementioned ritual, she did not flinch. Her skin was clammy, her breath shallow, her body barely more than an outline in his candlelight.

The wine and blood swirled thick as ink, as he dropped the nail and thorn inside. The incantations the Stranger had given him felt foreign on his tongue. Guttural, ancient syllables passed from one doomed soul to the next. As the words left his lips, the room, pregnant with unease, groaned as though something had taken notice.

He buried the bottle at the farthest corner of their land, packing the earth down hard with the heel of his boot. As he straightened, her howls carried on the wind; low and keening. A pressure settled in the air, thick as stagnant water. His vision thundered.

Inside, her body jerked violently, a convulsion that arched her spine and twisted her limbs into unnatural contortions. The sound that left her lips an unearthly, guttural rasp that was not her own. The air turned sour with the scent of her catamenia and spoiled milk.

After an extended struggle to separate the parts of herself that had been rapidly shifting into obscurity, she was no longer the shell she had been. Rejoicing the Stranger and the cures, the home was lighter, brighter - shadows lifted and joy returned. They agreed to find this Stranger and give thanks, fresh bread and wine for the return of the humble life they once held dear.

As they reached the Rowa, they were instead met with a neighbour, beside herself with grief. She fell to her knees and with a lamentable outcry, accused the two of the death of her husband.

"His final deathbed utterances were of you - you were seen on the threshold of his mind's clearing! It was your spirit rising from the dead and seeking to snare him with its chains! He was beckoned by a procession of daemons and witches, scouring for their next home! That is why I am languishing here, in the dark, mad, and wasting!"

The two were dumbfounded with the accusations.

"We were following the guidance of the Traveller, who claimed I would be set free of my woes with a simple collection, and ritualistic burial! Stuck in a constant conflict – what good was it if I were being driven to despair and suicide?

Far in the distance, a storm had been gathering. Dreary charcoal skies were dominated by clouds which spat ash and smoke into the air. Balls of black powder were cast up in time with the grim and inexorable march of a procession.

The head of the group, had bronze skin and copper hair, which accentuated the stark lines of a white face, bore the vermillion fabric of a tunic that exuded an almost hypnotic rhythm of its own; indeed the strange Traveller was the most striking of the crowd.

# AMANDA BLAKE
# SACRAFICIAL

So now the plague
has come to our door.
What have we done?
Do we not worship You
and do all we should do,
in the name of your Son?
Is there something more
to be or to become?

What of their home?
Not beauty, but grace
in pure smoother skin,
unmarked and unmarred
by rash or by scar.
What greater contrition
shown in what haste,
or what devil within?

In Your name, I give tithe.
I give You my alms.
In Your name, I give charity.
I raise to You psalms.
They do not remember
the Sabbath or keep it holy.
They do not remember You
or praise Your name only.
What greater sacrifice,

# SACRAFICIAL

what grander gesture show?
Are you asking for meat
instead of incense divine?
A more favored bloodline?
Offering of flesh more elite?
We only want to know
the best way to entreat.

Have this head of hare,
this brace of white lamb,
like the babe of Bethlehem,
unstained blood scarlet red.
We did what Scripture said,
yet it is us You condemn.
Now we try what we can—
more than can be said of them.

Make of our plague a sign.
Alleviate the burn of our pain.
Give succor from this endless ache.
Wash away our guilt and shame.
This pure sacrifice, without blame,
to Your scarlet lips we raise,
to consume their scorched stain.
Give now to us their grace.

How does body and blood smell now
in this black-boiled End of Days?

# STEPHEN HOWARD
# UNBOUND

You are their monument, though they do not know your name. They, over time, have called you many things, never touching on the truth. Not the leaders of armies, not the druids, not the witches. Nor the kings and queens or tribal leaders, despite the certainty of their convictions. They deal in absolutes, do humans.

And here she is again. The girl visits you in your forest clearing with growing regularity. Surrounded as you are by the dark green of thick conifers, she must travel a great distance to sit and talk with something that does not talk back, something she sees only as a monolith. She is older now, her skin taut. She crouches before you, knees nestling in your earth.

"He leaves in the night sometimes. Tells me not where he's going. He won't stay if I cannot bear child."

She places her hands on your cold stone. She would not if she knew. She would recoil.

While she resides in her own head, you wonder if she notices, if any of them ever notice, the silence. The trees are void of squirrels. Deer steer clear. Even the birds will not fly overhead. Animals always display better instincts than humans.

"Please bring me a child," she says, clasping her hands together.

With her prayers, her belief, you rise. A tremor shakes ferns and pinecones from the trees. Despite this, she stays for a long time, burying her fingers into your earth, speaking aloud her hopes and fears. They are simple in comparison to your own.

By the time she leaves, darkness prevails.

Their voices carry through the forest. One is loud but disinterested, complaining of sore feet and great distance, neither of which he truly comprehends. The other voice is soft and pleading, diminutive.

She holds bramble and thick shrubbery aside and he strides through without glancing back, without care for her. He strides toward you, throws his head to the left and spits, then stops.

"What is it you want from me, Sara?" he asks. His eyes are bloodshot, his odour stale and grainy.

She walks past him, to you, and lays a hand on you in the tender way she always does. The energy pours into you.

"It's what you want, what *I* can give to *you*." She turns to him, stalks over, lays her tender hand on his chest. "This place is sacred. Life-giving. There is creation here."

His hand moves to her hair, fingers intertwining with its auburn strands. He leans into her face, places his other hand on her stomach. "But is there creation in here?"

She moves to pull away, but he tightens his grip. "Is there?" he asks again.

She nods. "Lay with me. Here."

And so they lie together in the way humans do. The act is over quickly. You sense her faith, her certainty, and it provides you the impetus to break free. The ground shakes, the earth ruptures. He is pulling his clothes back on, stumbles and falls.

"Is that rock getting bigger?" he asks.

She, too, is dressing again. "Your eyes deceive you, my love. It is a sacred monument, a symbol of many things, all good."

"Should there not be markings then, arcane symbols of a sort?" he says, squinting at you.

"If there were, it would only indicate men had defiled it," she replies, stern, protective, enthralled.

He shrugs his shoulders and walks away, not holding the whip-like branches back for his wife. Not looking back at all.

✝

Her stomach is bloated, and she cradles it, one hand beneath the bump, one hand sat atop, as if carrying precious cargo. She is with child. This state is delicate, not one you expect her to make the journey to your clearing in. All is not well.

She scurries towards you but does not place her hand on you. She is distant. She keeps her distance.

"Still, he disappears at night. Still, he speaks ill of me. I give and give, for what?" She waves her hands, stomps back and forth. The anger in her is malign, useless to you.

"I should leave. That's what I should do. That'll show him." She stops marching and crouches down, her belly resting on her thighs.

There are others. They visit you from time to time, say a prayer, sing a song, prance around. But none come like she does, none *believe* like she does. If you are to succeed, you need her to stay.

You do what you can to disperse your presence, to trick the nature surrounding you. It takes time, but she sits with you, uttering her despairs, her hopes, her everything. Until, finally, a deer wanders into your clearing. They never come this deep into the forest because they know something isn't right. But this one is curious at what it deems your absence. It walks on uncertain legs, sniffs the ground, snorts and grunts. Gaining confidence, it walks up to her, nuzzles into her neck.

"Perhaps this is a sign," she says. "Thank you."

Your presence returns. The deer's head shoots up, eyes alert. It scampers away, kicking up dirt with its hurried hoof steps.

✝

Your strength returns, day by day, as if fuelled by unwavering belief. It is some time since her last visit, and you sense something is wrong.

A while later, she emerges from the darkness of the trees. Her body is different again, slimmer even than before the bump. Frail, pale, shadows under her eyes. Weary.

She lies down beside you, curls up into a ball. She lies like that until the sky dims and darkens and the stars you miss so dearly glint as if in invitation.

"How does one master loss?" she says in a quiet voice.

You cannot communicate with her, not in a way she can clearly understand. You can only listen.

"Why was this taken from me? I did everything right. I did everything right. Didn't I?" She whispers such questions over and over, the same questions humans always ask you, as they have done for centuries. Despite everything, they go on believing. Whatever answers they seek, they find.

"I must trust in the gods, in this place of theirs. I will not let this break me or my faith." She balls her hands into fists, holds them against her forehead. She sighs. In time, she falls asleep.

It is morning when she wakes, gathers herself, and returns home.

She is approaching. You can feel her footsteps from far away. She will not make it to you this time.

Her faith in you is misplaced, but your faith in her is rewarded. Either side of the forest, some distance from your revered head, your hands break ground. With the purchase you gain, fingers wrapping around thick trees, you pull yourself up and into the daylight. First, your full head comes through, right there in your peaceful clearing. Your shoulders next, ripping up the cedars, shattering your restraints. Soon, you haul your legs up from the depths of this ancient planet.

You are unbound.

She approaches still, viewing you in your full majesty. Her small village is surrounded by high walls. A prison, much like the earth is your prison. Was your prison. Only, they cannot free themselves, not in their current state.

She understands you as a sacred place, stationary, religious, but you are so much more, and there is so much more for you to see. Still, she approaches, awe and wonder dragging her onwards. Your perfect follower, her pain and desire dark clouds rendering her blind, obedient, servile. Behind her, villagers spill through the gates. Some flee, some carry flames. So typical. You stretch your legs, leaving this place, leaving her behind. When the night comes, you will look to those stars again, use them as your guide. There are ancient quarrels to pursue.

# ADAM HULSE
# LET ME TELL YOU ABOUT YOUR FATHER

On the eve of Christmas, I was awoken by a ghostly sob. My heart hammered a new tune.

"Leave him be!" I heard my aunt Maude cry.

Footsteps stumbled towards the bedroom where I had slept ever since my dear mother had passed two years ago. The door creaked open like a cat yawning, and I peered over my rough blankets at the silhouette swaying there in the gloom. For a moment, I felt a strange sensation as though I was looking at my father, whom I had only seen in the crumpled photograph I had inherited from my mother after the sickness had taken her. His ship had been lost to the sea shortly before my birth. The man in the doorway moved slightly so the oil lamp my aunt was carrying beat the shadows away to reveal my uncle Charles. I blinked sleepily, and inwardly cursed my foolishness. Of course, the man looked similar to his own brother, but he was shorter and did not possess the striking blue eyes my mother had told me so much about.

"Come with me, child," Charles slurred.

I was quick to throw my cold feet over the side of my bed, as I knew my uncle had a habit of being quick to lose his temper. Aunt Maude fussed in the background and when I searched out her eyes for reassurance, they looked away. Uncle Charles held his hand out for me to take, and although the gesture was not warm, I reached for it dutifully. My uncle's pinstriped suit was in disarray and his breath was hot with rum. While on the landing, he swayed so violently it felt as though the whole house was teetering and I swear my feet momentarily left the rug; the movement partnered with a sombre creak of wood.

*Is this a dream*? I fretted.

"Please, Charles," my aunt sobbed. "He's just a child."

With that, my uncle snatched the lamp from my aunt's hand and leaned close to her puffy face.

"I promised them!" he hissed. "Wait in our room if you must, but I will see this through."

My mind raced as my aunt disappeared behind a slammed door and I descended the stairs with my uncle. We finally stopped in the moonlit hall, and I jumped in fright as my bare feet hit an icy cold puddle of water. I could see it was running from under the door that led to the front parlour. My uncle lurched clumsily causing a splash of the water to hit me in the face. I was surprised to taste salt and that I was frozen in confused hesitation.

"Come now, boy," my uncle grunted while pulling at my arm.

The door opened to reveal the room, as I once knew it, had all but gone. In fact the very dimensions seemed to have changed as I felt the now familiar tilt pulling me one way and then another. Inexplicably the room was now flooded with grey looking water while ruin was all around. A gentle wave broke over my uncle and I before splashing up the damp walls of the hallway. I turned to look up at the face of my guardian for reassurance to steel me against the terror that bubbled within me. The sight of my uncle silently weeping made my legs buckle with fright. He sniffed once as though cold and waded out further into what had become of a once familiar room. Fog drifted up ahead so I could make little sense of what lay up ahead. I swear I could hear the mournful bell of a lone boat but the lapping of the water preoccupied my ears.

I froze once more but again the pull of my uncle's grip was too much for me to resist.

"Uncle, please," I pleaded. "I don't understand."

I was soon up to my waist in the frigid water that sloshed up the walls all around us. By now, we should surely have breached the boundaries of the house and I had expected to hit a wall many steps back. My uncle remained stony faced and silent. His breath was ragged with fear and I fought the urge to relieve my bladder right there in the water. I was about to resume my questioning when the sound of the bell began to toll all around us. Louder and louder it became until my uncle's freezing cold hand began to hurt my fingers under his fearful grip. The lamp flickered and failed and we were plunged into almost total darkness. Water still pressed against us, holding us with godly power. I whimpered and watched how moonlight broke through where I had believed the ceiling to be. It danced on the ripples of this impossible sea we found ourselves in. Uncle Charles let go of my hand for a moment and I felt the water try to pull me away.

"Uncle!" I cried out.

"Steel yourself, boy," came the reply as he tried to relight the lantern.

I teetered on the brink of falling forwards and then, just as suddenly, backwards. Something within me warned I would never rise back to the surface if I succumbed to the rising waves pulling at my ankles. The sea had visited the house and it wasn't about to soften its edges for a poor unfortunate such as myself. With one last desperate grunt, my uncle got the lantern burning again. His eyes filled me with dread, as they appeared hollowed out by an endless darkness. What I had mistook for drunkenness was actually a state of traumatic shock. Still, my uncle grabbed my arm and dragged me in his wake towards where the back parlour used to be. The door appeared swollen against its frame and the creak it emitted chilled my bones to the marrow. Even my uncle hesitated as he held the cold handle in his hand. He pressed his forehead into the panel and held it there. A tear ran down his nose and I watched it escape to the water that enveloped us.

"I'm sorry that I promised them such things," he wept before opening the door.

A man turned to watch our entrance. My teeth chattered at the sight of him as my knees threatened to dunk me below the water. There were shapes that moved unnaturally under the cape of his naval uniform as though the mist had been born there. My uncle wept openly before hurrying out of the room. I heard the sloshing sound of his retreat but couldn't turn my eyes away from the figure before me. The strange figure held his arms out for me and I found myself compelled to walk to him on legs fit for nothing more than a dream. Gurgling sounds came from his throat until they were as loud as the bell that clanged excitedly at my proximity. The shapes beneath the cape danced and reached out for me hungrily as I cursed my legs for their final betrayal. My father's striking blue eyes were dull now, but they took me in all the same.

# SASHA RAVITCH
# I WISH SPRING BREAK WOULD LAST FOREVER

A neck vein is pumping synchronously with a Bluetooth speaker's bass. Chad Renstrom, aka Chad R: blonde buzzcut with a grin saying, *"just exercising my second amendment rights, officer."* Chad R. moves through the world with confidence borne of the knowledge that he can say or do whatever he wants and his peers will respond with the same sycophantic enthusiasm found in evangelical churches and political rallies.

This wave of peers, clad in sleeveless shirts and low-rise jeans, crashes across main street. They are electrified by the flashing neon of 2D beer bottles and open-signs: a quivering, lustrous contour giving downtown an appearance of creeping hyperreality. Chad R. had insisted on St. Petersburg, Florida for their senior year Spring Break. They did not fight his choice; one doesn't insult God by asking him "why". It's close to the beach, the motels are cheap, and night managers don't ask questions.

"Okay, Florida, let's go!" Chad Bainbridge, aka Chad B. This is their way, their fraternal exegesis. From one Chad to another Chad, to a different Chad after that. A periodical proclamation of hype, a vibe-boosting sermon in ten syllables or less. They take turns passing the microphone of whatever bottle of booze they are pre-gaming, launching galvanizing chants into the o-zone to be heard by some still wakeful god.

"Man, this place *sucks*," Chad Littleton, aka Chad L., to his girlfriend, Mandy Anderson, aka Mandy A. "Bars close hella early and their beer tastes like Chad G's pre-workout piss."

"You should be so lucky, my brother," Chad Garrison, aka Chad G, crows over the heads of Mandy Yeats, aka Mandy Y., and Mandy Sanders, aka Mandy S.

"Imma 'boutta check out the beach," Chad L. calls out. Chad R., the alpha Chad, sets his square jaw in a grimace.

Chad R. shouts something over the clamor of the crowd, undermining Chad L.'s perceived coup and reaffirming his position as pack leader. Chad L. swallows hard but plays it cool, turning his face away from Mandy A. so she won't see his embarrassment. He just needs to walk this feeling off, as is the medicine of his kind.

The Chads and Mandys storm the beach, a kaleidoscope of polyester and outlet-mall psychedelia glowing beneath occasional streetlamps. Their teeming bodies are a ship rocking against waves of belligerent drunkenness and knowledge of their own fuckability. They collide as they navigate a sloping dune of sand leading down to the beach. It's darker here and the ocean is obscured by tall grasses.

"This is crop circle shit." Chad G.

"Like a fucking corn maze" Chad L.

The Mandys crowd single-file behind Chads creating spaces for the girls to crawl through, echoing some perennial genetic conditioning: intrepid explorers in a densely subtropical forest. This is simply DNA.

Chad R. calls out, and the group fights their way through the pampas grass to join him. Chads and Mandys meet an uninterrupted view: a long stretch of unpopulated sand which feeds into the mouth of an ocean illuminated by an otherworldly glow of luciferin.

"Wow, it's like, so magical." Whispers Mandy S., reverent.

"I wish Spring Break would last forever," replies Mandy Y. They look at each other, speaking a telepathic language, and begin running with exhilarated squeals toward the water. The Chads stampede after them, followed by the more timid Mandys who know to wait their turn.

Bottles of Jaeger and Captain Morgan circulate the sabbat-circle, the speaker flashing pink, then blue, then green, then orange, then yellow, then pink again, and blue again, a technicolor idol in the temple of young adult decadence. Skinny hips are colliding against the crinkling texture of swimming trunks. Slobbering kisses bloated with alcohol yeasts are making suckling sounds in tandem with the tide. A particularly enthusiastic Chad is rapping along to a song which has words he, a descendent of WASPS as white as the cocaine in his pocket, shouldn't feel so comfortable shouting.

It's paradise, it's perfect. Bodies, tan by both nature and design, swarm, slither, and slide against each other. It's such a good thing to be so young, so hot, so full of the raging thrum of purpose which animates perfectly sculpted limbs tossed hither and thither. It's such a good thing to know you are still so fuckable, even while puking up the technicolor sunset of your cocktail. It's so, so fucking good to be a Chad, to be a Mandy.

A Mandy wanders away like a cancer cell splitting off. This Mandy probably has a last name, but no one knows it. She's a transfer student from UC Santa Cruz, and she'll receive a surname-initial when she's earned it. Mandy the Surnameless gasps as she walks into the water and the bioluminescent algae tickles her ankles. These memories make Spring Break a monument of the Ideal in the suburban imagination. These memories will be revisited over and over again during alumni reunions, Labor Day and 4th of July BBQs, bachelorette parties, groomsmen toasts.

"Oh my god, it's like, so, *so* beautiful," Mandy A. joins her, leaning over and dragging orange polished nails through shimmering water. "It's literally amazing."

Soon they are all standing calves-deep in the uncanny glow of the ocean. Hoots and hollers perforate the thick canopy of night and its mantle of many winking, wandering stars. Salt water stings their eyes as Chads stomp around and splash Mandys, occasionally lifting one of the shrill–ly screaming girls and dunking her into the shallows. It's picturesque in the way that an Abercrombie & Fitch commercial lingers in your memory: white sands, white skin, white teeth, white collar.

Mandy the Surnameless stumbles. It's innocuous at first, observed by none of the others in their feral tumult. She sways slightly: a tall reed in a modest breeze, a captive audience at a soft rock concert, a cobra charmed by a flute. The world isn't spinning, but instead peeling from the walls of her reality in soft, wet, downward-wagging tongues. These soft, wet tongues are illumined in the same phosphor-blue of the seawater staining her skin. She somehow recalls the caves her family visited in New Zealand, where glow worms hung suspended from a cavernous ceiling in stalactites of lambent mucus.

"Guys, I feel…" Mandy the Surnameless bends over the surface of the water and retches up a river of thick, neon blue puke.

"Oh my god, *gross*, this is so fucking gross!" Mandy A. leaps backwards, stumbling into Chad R. who subsequently knocks Chad L. onto his ass in the water, bringing several others tumbling down with him.

Mandy the Surnameless heaves more thick blue slime up. The world is blooming in sharp fractals of nameless beauty before the infirm twenty year old. Her eyes are wide and wicked as she watches the glowing, growing mass of her vomit melt into the pulsating algae in fearsome and flowering shapes. Faces appear in the crucibles of these fluorescing flowers, stretching and melting, contorting into wretched nostrils hollowing themselves out into eyes which burn with the green of a comet's tail. She counts the outline of cracked molars sprouting from shifting, shaking lines staring back at her through her own reflection.

Her eyes will not focus, but if they could, she would notice swathes of her skin which have made contact with the water are puffing up like marshmallows in a microwave. What she cannot not see, however, she can certainly feel. Her body is possessed of pins and needles: a feverish prickling. Mandy's fingers flex into claws. She begins to scratch.

An echo of hateful gurgling passes through the Chads, the noises sticking in their throats and falling out of their mouths. Chad L. and Chad G. lean on each other as seething blue bile erupts from their many orifices with the sticky viscosity of melted candy. Chad G. brings his vape to his mouth and his lips birth a thick wave of topaz vomit, a plume of cotton candy flavored smoke hovering above it like sea foam. "Dude," he sputters, a stupefied grin tugging at only one corner of his neon-spittle stained lips.

"Dude," Chad L. replies, one of his arms stretched heavenwards like an apostle, like a martyr of God awaiting his judgment. Chad L. is throttled by reverence, gazing up at the wrathful glory of a sky split open to reveal a thousand trembling black palms, their fingers probing the soft carcass inside his skull. "Yo, God is so real for this," he whispers, falling to his knees in the water as his bones begin gelatinizing under the pressure of devotional piety.

It is then that the thing in the water finally gets Chad R., his eyes corrupted by a sickening supernal luster which shines as mean and as blue as his blood. He strides deeper into the water until it takes him up to his hips, his fingers creating new geometry amidst incandescent effluvia. He is feeling his flesh bloat, swelling with pustules and twitching blisters. Blisters pregnant with luciferin blue. Blisters pulsing with their own individual heartbeats stolen from the core of dying stars. Blisters shaking with each step, gravid and gross. As they become too swollen to cleave to the melting candle wax of his skin, they slough off into the sea with a nauseating plunk. There, these placental sacks dissolve, revealing microscopic swarms of mellifluous creatures. The egg sacks of arachnid-fish, milky gelatinous eyes with legs of orb-weavers, disappear beneath the water.

A choir of rancid hymnals are raining down from the heavens upon the engorged and trembling flesh of youth. The words are not discernible, but the dialect is universal: tongues made of skyiron unraveling supernal ecstasy inside the growing lumps of young adult bodies. A cacophony of moans underpins the violent music of retching and scratching, of skin flaying and melting, of teeth being plucked from jawbones and offered to glowing waves. The Chads and Mandys are being swept up, over and over, in the collective orgasm of their unbodied agony, distended bellies and liquid limbs stumbling toward each other in mindless hunger. Perfect still, perfect always, perfect flesh sagging from bones melting more by the moment, flags of curdled white and glowing blue flown at half mast.

Chad R. is the last to join them: an inflated sack of pallid meat gazing with glutted eyes at the sky. The things below in the water have made him into a revenant of the things above. He witnesses as flaming constellations repattern themselves into the shape of a toothless maw, an event horizon of unabated appetite. As if this is a long awaited cue, Chad R. nods and turns to join the quivering amalgam of his peers.

He drags the puddling bags of his body through the shallow tide toward his classmates. Had his eyes been capable of seeing plainly, he would surely have torn them out. Before him shivers the undulating ouroboros of his peers, white as the moon and blue as the stain from the water. Rotting and ruptured hands jamming into what were once mouths, feet breaking backwards and hooked into ears, heads fully submerged in weeping and prolapsing rectums, and all the while the heavens singing a tribute to their beauty. Chad R. feels tears of awe and adoration force their way out of what remains of his tear ducts as he reaches the coagulating conclave. With the last of his bodily autonomy, he flings himself into their party.

Chad R. erupts, the pregnant abscess of his body meeting the mouths and moans of the mass, his sloughing remains assimilating with ease and erasing his individuality. What unprecedented bliss has met the unwitting denizens of youth upon these hallowed shores. What benediction immortalizes them in the annals of the awful stars. In unctuous, wet, and slapping rotations the Spring Breakers, the collective Chad and Mandy, navigate its way to shore. Slowly, slowly, it climbs the beach toward the town, with one thought only in its shared mind: *I wish spring break would last forever.*

# WIEBO GROBLER
# THE GUARDIAN

The bruised sky roiled and boiled, dark toxic clouds filled with flashes of white and deep menacing shadows disguising the celestial battle being fought up high.

An eternal battle has raged through the covens in an endless cycle for as long as he can remember. Back when they were the mediators, trying and failing to appease the constant flux of petty conflict, when they were worshipped and called upon to guide and bless from holy cairns and ancient monoliths that channelled the heavenly fire.

Refusing to pick a side, they were eventually exiled from the heavens and cast down to earth to dwell deep beneath the oceans. An injustice for sure, but not surprising. Demons can't be trusted, and angels are pedantic assholes. No longer able to heed the calls of their celebrant's the rituals of old were lost, the cairns broken the monoliths toppled.

He could sense the coming battle—he had for days—every pore tingling, and a dull throbbing ache building up behind his eyes. Pressure upon the pressure of the crushing depths where they dwelled. He was restless, concerned about the inevitable fallout.

His mate wrapped her arms around him. She didn't have to follow him down here, into the darkness, but she did. He squeezed her back, his color changing, brightening. She was and always has been his strength in this ever-cold and constant dark place where no light or warmth from the sun reached the crevices of their new home.

He disengaged himself from her embrace and slowly drifted up from the ravine, the currents tugging and pulling at his body. Light from the world above filtered down as black became grey, inky indigo became aquamarine. He passed beautiful rows of coral reefs, home to an array of wonderful creatures. The water turned turbulent as he neared the surface. His sensitive skin picked up the most minuscule instabilities of power and electricity. Small blue sparks of static jumped across his body like racing seahorses. His eyes, the size of shields, broke the surface, and a wall of noise assaulted him.

The wind howled like a banshee, herding the waves like a demented shepherd and gleefully driving them to smash against the cliffs near the shore in thundering crashes.
High above, the rumble and crack from the battle raging in the clouds added to the chaos. Ribbons of light pulled curtains of water across the pewter sky.

Straight ahead, he saw one of the beautiful wood and canvas birds struggling through the squall. Its shapely breast lifted high above the waves before slamming back down in a violent spray of white.

This bird was large. Larger than any he'd seen before. The two sets of tall and rigid white wings on its back swayed from the impact. He lifted himself out of the water, his skin a kaleidoscope of shifting colors and patterns. A calming hue of blue with white dots to represent the summer sky.

As big as the bird was, he still towered above it. The small parasites onboard screamed and pointed as he loomed over them. Tiny flowers of fire bloomed from the end of dead sticks held to their shoulders. Pretty little displays of orange and yellow light which he always enjoyed.

A stray spear from the celestial battle fell from the skies. A jagged white-hot fork of light struck one of the wings with a blinding crack, splitting it in half and setting fire to the bird's plumes.

He roared in anger, and a maelstrom of bubbles emerged from his mouth. His skin changed to scarlet, and black lines pulsated across its surface like living ink.

The demons were not playing fair. They wouldn't give him a chance. How was he supposed to protect these creatures from the dangers of the sea, if they wouldn't allow him to do his job? He was a Guardian now. Self-sworn to warn these beautiful creatures away from smashing into the rocks and running themselves into the jagged reefs hidden beneath the waterline.

Tentacles flailing like whips, he smacked at the flames, sending parasites cartwheeling through the air to be swallowed by the violent waters. But just like Midas, his touch was a curse. Kraken, leviathan, monster. Names he did not deserve. The suckers on his tentacles tore large chunks from the bird. He plucked a few of the parasites from the water, but themselves being such delicate little things, he held them too tight, and they turned purple before exploding in sprays of hot red liquid.

He gently tried to lift the stricken bird from the water, but something in its belly ignited, and with a bright flash, the bird disintegrated.

He felt sorry for the parasites as they clung to the broken pieces of their host, mewling at the sky. Soon, they would join her like so many others, carried along by the strong currents and strewn across the seabed like white bloated starfish.

He took one last look at the battle still raging above before sinking back down to join his mate.

From his coloring and the overwhelming sadness in his eyes, it was clear that he'd failed once again.

She couldn't tell him that it was pointless. Just another trick those above chose to play on him and his naïve notion of duty. He had to have a purpose. Or he would become still, his beautiful colors would fade, and he would become translucent until, finally, he would disappear.

# DAVID MITCHELL
# DAWNS MEYN

Screams pierced the crisp Cornish night as nineteen pyres were erected around the Lamorna's town square. Two figures, young men with floppy hair and chiselled jaws, cried out until their throats burned and their chests heaved. All before a single ember had been lit.

The whole town, and some from further afield, folk from Mousehole, Sennen, and St Buryan, had all come out to see the purging of the 'Merry Maidens'. Sinful women who had dared to dance on the Sabbath. Harlots who had, in their succubus ways, also lured two of the town's best and brightest men, to cavort with them. Snakes with apples.

"PLEASE, PLEASE, ARE YOU ALL MAD!?" screamed one of the boys, wrestling himself free from the grips of one of the townsfolk. He was not bound, nor gagged, he wasn't here to be punished tonight. This was a lesson. He was a naïve victim. "WE WERE DANCING. WE WERE SINGING." The boy sobbed and paced, he implored the crowd, one person at a time, but no one would meet his gaze. "THAT IS ALL! IS MUSIC NOT THE LORD'S WORK?"

A sceptre swiftly smashed into the lad's face. A wash of blood, and at least one tooth, dashed the cobbled streets. He fell to the floor, and wept into its harsh surface, shedding tears, blood, and phlegm, in equal measure.

"Now, now, boy. Our Lord is forgiving, but even he has limits."

Father Jowan inspected the end of the gold sceptre in his hand and grimaced, before pacing towards the sobbing pile of tears and blood, and wiping the sceptre clean on its shirt.

"Ladies and gentlemen!" The voice boomed and rippled in the air, full of theatre and gravitas. The clergyman revelled in his role of speaker, judge, and executioner. "We have gathered here tonight to do the lords work!" He flounced as he spoke, wafting his arms and swinging the sceptre around.

"BRING OUT THE CONDEMNED." He bellowed, as he stretched his arms out wide.

In silence – bar the frenzied wailing of the two youngsters - a surly, thick man, with tired eyes and leathery skin, led a procession of nineteen bound women into the town centre. The women had sacks atop their heads, and one-by-one they were unlinked from the chain, and led to their individual bonfires, and affixed to a stake at their top.

Into each stake there was a carving;

"The righteous will be glad when they are avenged, when they bathe their feet in the blood of the wicked. Then men will say, 'surely the righteous still are rewarded; surely there is a God who judges the earth'." Psalm 58:10, 11

When the last of the women were bound to wood, Father Jowan approached the surly man and kissed him on the forehead.

"Well done, with Christ, with Christ."

And then shoo'd the man away, the Father didn't share his stage.

"The RIGHTEOUS, will be glad, when they bathe their feet in the BLOOD of the WICKED" His cadence was off-beat, he sped up, and slowed down, at odd times, and randomly emphasised words. He was captivating but unsettling, and a rare fire burned in his eyes. "THE TORCHES!!!"

Father Jowan dramatically pointed his sceptre in a crescent, making sure to aim at each of the women and their pyres. Nineteen dark figures emerged from the shadows, holding long-handled torches, their faces hidden beneath hooded cloaks.

"NOOOOOOO." A feeble scream from a worn throat.

The second of the boys had broken free, although in truth, the grip on him had become little more than a tender grasp.

He sprinted towards a pyre in the middle of the arc, and mounted the mass of branches and twigs. He removed a sack to reveal a flash of bright chestnut hair. A fair, freckled woman smiled weakly, through bloodstained lips.

"It's going to be okay." She mouthed, but little sound came out.

The boy simply held the girl and wept.

"Hahahaha." The Priest's voice dominated the square once more. "The boy is on to something there. We need to be able to see the Lord's work in action. REMOVE THEIR HOODS." He laughed wickedly again, expecting the crowd to echo him, but he got little more than a gentle murmur back.

Reluctant townsfolk came forward and removed the girl's hoods. Many whispering soft prayers and comforts as they did so, before shrinking back into the anonymous crowd.

The Priest's breaths were becoming frantic. Spittle pooled in the corners of his mouth and the nethers of his robes grew tighter.

"PUUUURGGGE THEM." He screamed, gesturing towards the pyres.

"But what about the boy?" yelled a concerned female voice, from deep within the crowd.

"He-he-he will repent, and join the flock..." Father Jowan pirouetted on the spot, waving his sceptre joyously around him. "...or he will burn."

The boy who'd been beaten and berated got to his feet. He wiped the blood from his face and calmly walked to the nearest pyre, hopping atop, wrapping his arm around a small blonde girl with bleary eyes. Cries and screams rippled from one side of the crowd.

In a calm, but firm voice he spoke.

"If this is God's work then let me burn too, for I long to meet a creator who allows such things, to vent my mind."

The statement was met with cries and gasps in equal measure.

"BLASPHEMY. THE DEVILS TONGUE IS COATED SILVER!" The priest screamed over the rumblings of the crowd.

Casting his sceptre to the floor he grabbed one of the torches, and lit the pyre below the bleeding boy. "May you burn in hell…"

"…and may you, ALL OF YOU, REMEMBER THIS NIGHT, SO LONG AS ALL YOUR WRETCHED LIVES MAY LAST." The boy's bleeding head was held high, defiant.

In an uncharacteristically uncontrolled moment, Father Jowan began sprinting, he ran between each pyre lighting them frantically. He then began ripping the other torches from the statuesque townspeople's hands, and tossing them onto the fledgling fires.

"NOW, A PRAYER!" The Priest suggested, adjusting his – now – dishevelled robes, in an attempt to regain his composure. "Our Father…."

"Our Father…" The crowd mumbled back, instinctively.

"Who art in heaven…"

"Who art in heaven…"

A piece of wood crackled, and popped, and screams and cries erupted from the crowd. The flames were now licking at the feet of the condemned.

"HALLOWED BE THY NAME."

Nothing was returned but mumbles and cries.

"HALLOWED. BE. THY. NAME." Thundered Father Jowan.

The crowd offered nothing back, but from the fires came a lone, soft voice. The girl with the beaten lips and chestnut hair began to sing, in high, angelic tones.

"The first time I met you, my darling
Your face was as fair as the rose,
But now your dear face has grown paler
As pale as the lily white rose."

Her fragile voice overpowered the crackling of the flame, the cries of the crowd, and the booming tones of the clergyman. It cut through the smoke, and wounded all in attendance.

The priest and the crowd were stunned to silence, as one voice became many. Though their flesh bubbled and burned, their words rang out, clear and pure.

"I love the White Rose in its splendour

I love the White Rose in its bloom

I love the White Rose so fair as she grows.

It's the rose that reminds me of you."

The soft harmony continued to sing, unwavering, as the flames engulfed the pyres entirely. Not one voice broke, or cracked from its gentle velvety melody, not even as their black forms crumbled in the flames. But there was no second verse, and the chorus was never repeated.

The crowd stood, haunted faces illuminated brightly by the 'purging flame', in silent awe, as the flames slowly diminished.

"AMEN." Father Jowan spat, as the last of the orange glows died down. Sceptre again, now in his hand, as he turned to crowd, and pointed at them as if it were a blade. "AMEN." He repeated, with expectant eyes.

The crowd yielded, and gave the meek response "Amen," before shuffling off towards their homes. It had been a long night, and light was beginning to break on the horizon.

"The people who were in the dark saw a great light, and those in the land of the shade of death did the dawn come up!" exclaimed the priest, to the backs of people's heads, before smiling, and sauntering towards the field which kept his chapel.

†

Father Jowan awoke the next day feeling content. Last night had not gone by without its problems, but in the long term all that would be remembered was God's cleansing flame, and the purging of the unclean and unfaithful from his flock.

He donned his day robes, drab brown things, and left the chapel with the intention of going into town to see if the butcher and baker would supply him with enough tithes to make a nice lunch.

Inches from his front porch he was greeted by a large, sturdy stone pillar. The stone was approximately five-foot tall and two-foot wide, it must have weighed a tonne, but the ground showed no sign of disturbance and he'd heard no commotion in the night.

Many of the townsfolk had gathered outside the house, and the crowd was growing with each moment.

"What is the meaning of this?" Father Jowan barked. "What are you all gawking at?" He asked as he slid past the pillar, and towards the crowd.

With some distance between himself and the chapel, he was finally able to see. The pillar by his front door was just one of many. Nineteen pillars, of similar but not identical proportions, arranged around the chapel in a perfect circle. Just as with the first, the ground beneath each stone was completely undisturbed. It was as if the stones had always been there.

†

Despite publically repeating, "God moves in mysterious ways." Father Jowan had privately tried to have the pillars removed, again and again. But, each time he did so, grave misfortune befell those tasked with the job of moving them.

In the following year after the burning of the Merry Maidens, and the emergence of the Dawns Meyn (Dance of Stones), as they became known, three workers were crushed by winches collapsing, another six fell ill and never recovered, and two were even hit by lightning, on separate occasions. By their second year, no one was willing to take up the job, despite the high price the priest was willing to pay.

Father Jowan himself, had also began to change. His focused wrath had become blurred and confused. He was easily startled, and his sermons often petered out into nonsensical waffle, as if the Father was distracted by voices. He was often heard muttering about the 'infernal white roses' that called to him.

†

On the second anniversary of the Burning of the Merry Maidens, the town of Lamorna was a hubbub, overnight, each house had received a note, telling them to meet at the chapel at dusk, for a special sermon. The threshold for hubbubs is quite low in deep, dark Cornwall.

The town did as they were told, and congregated outside the chapel as the light faded.

The air carried a foul acrid smell, but otherwise the townsfolk were simply greeted by the familiar chapel, and increasingly familiar stones.

Father Jowan crawled out of an upstairs shutter, and climbed onto the roof, waving a torch.

"IS THIS IT? IS THIS WHAT YOU WANT?" he boomed, without it being clear whom he was addressing, and with a wavering, weak voice he began to sing.

"Now I am alone my sweet darling
I walk through my garden and weep
But spring will return with your presence
Oh lily white rose, mine to keep."

And with that he dropped his torch.

The oil in which the chapel was doused in caught quickly.

The chapel burnt with bright purging white flames.

**AUTHORS NOTE**

*The White Rose, which part of appears in this story is a Cornish Funeral song, and the Dawns Meyn are a rock formation in South West Cornwall. The origin myth is actually that 19 women were turned to stone, for the audacious act of dancing on the Sabbath, but a fiery change adds a little spice.*

104

# RYAN DAY
# HYDROLITH

The ceiling seethes before your eyes. Endless shifting patterns of darkness. Your eyelids close, popping back open like broken rain-shutters.

It's so hot tonight. The hottest night of the year.

The bedsheets are like cellophane smothering your skin.

Your thoughts boil in your skull. Steaming anger. There's an icy bottle of champagne sitting in the refrigerator. It would cool you down nicely. But the thought of it turns your stomach. Your bottle of celebration fizz. Now what is there to celebrate? An idiot could see you deserved the promotion – which makes your boss worse than an idiot.

Totally enraging.

You toss aside the damp sheets and climb out of bed.

You left the curtains open like usual. It doesn't matter, there's privacy enough to allow it. The moonlight streaming through paints the moisture on your skin blue.

The gardens in this neighbourhood are long and narrow like Dutch buildings, divided by monstrous hedgerows resistant to human intervention. Your boundary cuts off in a deep thicket of ensnarled vegetation with a natural pond nestled at its heart, just visible from the bedroom window.

Tonight, something out there catches your eye. A peculiar pale shape slouching through the undergrowth.

You watch the slow movements, tearing up clods of entangled grass and bursting brittle twigs. Your unblinking eyes stinging with tiredness as the moonlight unveils the shape to be a man. Stark naked, hairless, and as ghostly white as if his skin were made of meringue.

# RYAN DAY
## HYDROLITH

He crawls to the pond, dipping his head to lap at the scummy water. Slurping up big gulps of pond-brine as you observe motionless from the window.

The following night sees you once again counting the writhing mass of black worms on the bedroom ceiling. A room like a blacked-out sauna. The baked air leeches the sweat from your body. It turns to sap, gluing the sheets around you like a cocoon.

You were stuck at the office until late. The extra peoplepower needed to wade through the transitional backlog from the promotion that should have been yours. The cruel, infuriating audacity of it.

Arid eyes fixed on the ceiling, you attempt to cool down. Picturing frozen lakes and snowy tundra. But the ice melts beneath your simmering glare.

You forgot about the strange man you saw last night drinking from the pond. Or thought you saw. The memory is a heat-soaked blur now.

You shed the bedsheets like a bloated python and stagger to the window. You don't expect to see any albino men on all-fours, but it's not like you can sleep and it kills five minutes.

But when you look down your heart stops. Chills cruising through your spine.

The naked man is back. And this time he isn't alone. Men, women and children, equally pale and equally naked, crawl through the undergrowth to crowd around the pond. Jostling like antelope at a watering hole. Limbs like curdled-milk tentacles knotting together.

The scene unfolding is too mind-bogglingly macabre to bear looking at.

You close the curtains but don't return to bed.

Morning comes and your bones ache with sleepless fatigue.

Sunlight dapples the hedgerows in innocent gold and there is no sign of the nocturnal intruders. Dressed in just your slippers and bathrobe, you head outside bolstered by the courage of daylight. The dew clasping the overgrown blades of grass kisses your bare ankles.

At the bottom of the garden, where the manicured lawn and wild beyond meet, the pond is bone dry.

A dusty pit strewn with withered vegetation. Buried in the centre is a rock. A pink and glossy lump incongruous with its surroundings.

You reach down and take it out. It feels damp to the touch, but your palm remains dry. It is about the size of an apple, coarse like steel-wool and marked all over with deep crags.

You regard the rock in the sunlight, a prize jewel shimmering like a rose-tinted lagoon in your hand. It's still in your hand when you return inside.

An empty wasteland expands to every horizon. Endless dead earth beneath your feet. The sky above is a void. A white nothing drained of all colour. Every breath dries out your mouth and feels powdery in your throat.

As you wander, the dirt becomes sand. Creeping over your shoes. Swallowing your knees. A sucking pit emerging from nowhere. The earth claiming you, dragging you down to the depths of its stomach.

You are waist-deep before you think to scream. Wailing, churning your throat bloody from the grit in the air. You thrash until you are completely bound. Sand pours into your mouth. Plugs your ears and nostrils. A great smothering hand choking you blind…

You jolt awake. The only sound is the sweat dripping off your face onto the pillow. Steady tip-taps synchronising with your heartbeat.

The gaping desolation of the nightmare drained more than a few hours of sleep gave.

The rock sits clasped in your hand. With it, flashes of the desolate wasteland. Why does it feel as if that harrowing place exists not within your mind, but without? The furtive shame of a trespasser grips you.

The inside of your mouth feels chalky with dirt. You've never felt so thirsty.

Throwing a bathrobe around your clammy, uncomfortable skin, you head downstairs to the kitchen. At the sink, with your hand on the cold tap, a sight through the open blinds makes you jump. The empty glass in your other hand slips loose, shattering like an almighty shutter-click capturing the moment: the man on the other side – naked, hairless, whiter than a summer cloud – sucking the beads of condensation off the outside of the windowpane.

Quietly, carefully, you close the blinds and back away. Ears perked up like a rabbit in a wide-open field. Retreating all the way to the living room, where you park up on the sofa, knees pulled close to your chest.

Here, you wait for morning to come.

Another laboriously empty day ends, and you find yourself back in the wasteland. Wandering through apocalyptic bleakness until once again falling prey to the quicksand. You were so careful this time, watching your every step, but the earth outsmarted you. Dragging you down by the ankles and gobbling you whole.

Instead of waking, the dream carries you further and further until your eyes clear and a subterranean cavern materialises around you. Sand cascades down the walls like a persistent beige waterfall. Your footfalls echo loudly on parched rock. Every surface is sapped of lustre, drained of life, rendered dry as old chalk.

Deeper and deeper into the abyss…

Until a booming crash wrenches you awake. The cavern replaced with your dark, stuffy bedroom.

The house is lit up by crashing and banging coming from somewhere below. It sounds like the kitchen.

Your adrenaline-charged legs are unsteady as you sneak downstairs. Each fresh noise causes your muscles to lock-up momentarily.

The white people are here.

Inside the house.

The kitchen windows have been shattered. Glass shards on the counter like milky pebbles in the moonlight. One of the naked men is sprawled across the draining board. Colourless lips locked around the tap, cheeks sucking, throat undulating with massive gulps of water.

A naked woman crawls across the floor through to the passageway leading to the back door. Your coat is still wet from the drizzly journey home. Beads of moisture dappling the slick material. The droplets are like catnip. She pulls herself up, stretching out the sleeves, lapping the wetness from your coat.

Something stings the back of your calf and makes you recoil.

There is a baby thing on the floor, scampering around after you like an excitable puppy. A purple mouth-sized welt rises above your left ankle, oozing blood. The baby's scarlet-stained lips blow raspberries. Giggling voicelessly as it chases you around the kitchen.

You contemplate punting the creepy baby out the window like a match-winning field goal, but a better idea comes to you just in time.

As the ghouls ransack the kitchen for every miniscule drop of water, you race back upstairs. Into the bedside drawer. Returning to the kitchen with the pink rock clenched in your hand. The creeps – three indoors and more gathering to join the party outside the smashed window – stop what they are doing, all attention turning to you and the rock.

The nervous sweat on your face glints like stardust in their eyes.

You pull your arm back and launch the rock through the window as far as you can down the garden.

White heads swivel like disturbed bowling pins, tracing the pink arc through the darkness.

Then they begin to move. Those outside turning to amble away. The nightmare family in your kitchen retreating over broken glass and clambering back out through the mess they made.

You watch until the last ghostly-white form is swallowed by the shadows.

And then you watch some more.

Just in case.

You are so tired, sitting in the office, that your vision is a fuzzy blur of black and red mist. It hurts to blink. Carpet-tacks on the insides of your eyelids. It feels like someone has stabbed a straw in the base of your spine and sucked out your soul.

Ears blazing with static as your boss drones on. Mouth flapping. Teeth grey and irregular. An odious Stonehenge.

Angry bees buzz louder and louder in your skull.

A thrumming pulse vibrates your bones.

Some titanic force calling to you from deep underground.

Can anyone else feel it?

The next thing you know there is a stapler in your hand and your boss is missing their two front teeth. You are fired before they even mop the bloodstains off the whiteboard.

But it's good.

It's all good.

More time to try and sleep.

The arid cavern is a brown artery descending to the heart of the earth. Sand like aeons of shed skin sluices down the incline with you, pooling around your shoes. You can feel the booming breaths of whatever awaits below in your own chest.

Descending until you come out into an enormous subterranean chamber. Here the sand has gathered into an ancient pit. A colossal hourglass.

Standing proud in the centre is a rock as big as a skyscraper. A glossy pink monolith. Drawing moisture from the world around it. Draining rock and dirt to ruin. Fat beads of water crying down its smooth surface.

Even you aren't safe from its thirst. Feeling the liquid in your body being filtered out through your pores.

The rock calls to you. Filling your head with delirium. Wherever you are is a place that transcends mortal fears. You are a willing victim. Near-orgasmic as you let the weeping monolith feed on your life-force.

Its tears are stained crimson. The blood of the planet percolating through primeval strata.

You reach out.

A new day is born wearing a wreath of immaculate sunlight. The streets this morning awash with vibrant colour and summer cheer. Streets you stroll without a care in the world. The air tastes like cherry pie. The scents of hope and fulfilment caress your nose.

You have only taken the route you are walking once before. But you couldn't get lost if you tried. Indelible knowledge carved into your brain.

Once you arrive at your destination, you slow to a crawl. Just another rubbernecker on the scene, taking your place between the curiously gawping old people and the young people observing through the detached veil of phone cameras. Mesmerised by the dance of blue lights from emergency vehicles crowding the largest house on the street.

The bottom windows are shattered. The front door bashed to large splinters.

You loiter long enough to see the people in bright coats wheel out a gurney. Navigating through the dense throng of onlookers to the open doors of a waiting ambulance.

You recognise the body by its two missing front teeth. The rest is a mummified husk. Skin shrivelled like grey papier-mâché wrapped around their skeleton. Eyeballs withered to raisins. Lips receding into the jawbone.

Following the paramedics, a police officer steps out through the debris in the doorway, something apple-sized clutched in their hand. Sparkling like a pink diamond. Crying blood.

# J D M YODER
# LAMENTATIONS

O God, O God! Why hath thou forsaken me-- Deep beneath the ruins of the earth, where lay the partitions of all mankind, I stand like a fool of the Lord's own choosing. A jester to warn those moronic souls of the passing of all things to come, and all things of which have come before. They look upon my pitiful being, and they point their wretched fingers upon me as I dance and sing and ward them from perdition. Yet it is all to no avail. They stand before the precipice of endless torment, and I can do naught but watch them trot gleefully forward.

O Lord, O Lord, why hath thou abandoned me-- Was I not a good and faithful servant? A man who stood proud at your side? A harbinger of your will? Why now in this bleak abyss do you leave me to rot and fester, surrounded by my tormentors? What sin have I committed? What crime have I enacted? Was I born a hopeless, wretched thing that I have been cast away so spitefully? Was this always a fate to befall me?

O God, O God, what do these visions mean-- Why do I gaze long into this land of shadow and death, and see a world so beautiful and darling? A land of milk and honey, where suffering is no longer. Is this my punishment for a lifetime of loyalty? To see that eternity of which I was promised in my most miserable days, and know that I shall never obtain it? What twist of fate. What terrible recompense. I am no beast, no monster. I am a good and faithful servant, beholden only to you!

O Lord, O Lord, what trials must I overcome-- An existence beyond reckoning, sleeping in a bed of nails, and waking to a room of mirrors. Their laughter torments me. I can hear it in dreams most joyous and most wicked alike. It haunts

113

me until my senses can take no more, and remains there even when I jolt awake. Is this what awaits the most twisted of sinners? Those horrid men who stray from your light? When you molded me from clay, and breathed your life into my heart, is this always what you saw of me? Was this always my fate?

Then I shall do as I am commanded, for I am a good and faithful servant. I shall watch from the abyss and I shall play the tune that brings their laughter. I shall stand before these obelisk gates, and I shall dance in the light of their stygian hue. I will guard them with my life and allow no good man through. Those who laugh, who taunt, who push and pull and cast stones at me, I shall welcome them with open arms like brothers.

Then I shall watch them as they wilt in hellfire, subject to the whims of cruel Leviathan. And when they cry out to me, and they look for me, and when they seek out my cold embrace, I will not be there to cool them. I will not spit upon them. I will only gaze from my place as your good and faithful servant, and I shall never allow them to see those streets of gold and those clouds of ivory. This shall be my kingdom upon a hill, and none shall conquer it.

O God, O God, your purpose is my life-- I shall not forsake you. I shall never forsake you. I will do all that you have commanded, and I will lust not for your glory. I will become an ugly and homely thing, and I will remain here for endless eons until the day my services are no longer needed. I shall become a mighty and terrible thing, which fills all sinners with horror. When they look upon me they shall gaze upon their eternal soul, and know that they have wasted their lives, just as I have wasted mine.

O Lord, O Lord, I shall become the beast which you desire.

# JONATHAN HART
# THE WATCHERS

We watch in silence. We are the old ones; the ones who have always been here. The others work below us, their faces streaked with mud and sweat. The thud of mattocks biting into the cold clay echoes in the wet skies above like the lament of the dead.

The ones in the pit below us dig steadily, their labours broken by occasional jokes.

Laughter is shared, but we do not smile. We only watch and wait, wondering why they have come to this place between laces, why they dare disturb this hallowed ground. Perhaps they pray to new gods. If so, they are mistaken in their beliefs, for this ground was sacred even when we were young, and that was long ago.

A shovel strikes something, and the others bend down to examine their discovery.

There is a stir of excitement and then sighs: a stone. One of them casts it from the pit like so much rubbish, and it lands by our feet on the cut edge above his head. We say nothing, but we know the significance of this stone, the reason it was placed in the pit. The thing it was meant to hold in its chthonic cradle for an eternity.

And though we remain silent, the tension in our bodies is so strong that one of the diggers below straightens and peers up to where we stand. Her eyes narrow as she squints at the leaden sky, but she sees only the scudding clouds and wheeling crows.

Another scraping noise reverberates around the damp pit walls, and now we crane forward, our eyes burning with excitement. We watch as you kneel on the wet clay, deep below the ground we stand on. Deep enough to bury memories and time. Deep enough to bury the past. Casting aside your tools, you scrape at the earth clinging to the object, your friends crouching, their eyes expectant. We hardly need to see what it is you've uncovered. We know, for we have guarded this place for over four thousand winters.

As the clay crumbles beneath your fingers, you expose something smooth and white, and we look down with curious eyes, having never seen it like this. There are murmurs from your friends, but you are lost in your own little universe of excitement, peeling away the earth, exposing your find to the weakly dying light of the Winter sun.

And now it stares up at us. Do those empty sockets hold reproach? Anger? In their last moments, the eyes that sat there were wide with terror, but we know you understood. Everything has its place within the Great Cycle: its time of planting, its time of growth, its time of harvest.

You stand to confer with your friends, and we watch you gesture. One of them points to the darkening sky and shrugs, and you raise your voice at him, jabbing your hand towards the skull at your feet. The argument is brief. The others leave, but you stay, bending to your task. We say nothing, but we acknowledge your dedication. Perhaps, long ago, you could have been one of us.

We watch as you work, stripping clay from the skeleton as if you are removing flesh to expose shoulders, ribs, arms and then legs until the body, still in its foetal position, is exposed at your feet. You pause then, looking down at the skull, perhaps trying to imagine her face. No doubt you feel alone here, abandoned by your friends and left at the bottom of this shaft with a dead woman you never knew. You are not alone, though. We are here, just as we were those many moons past when we first placed her at the base of this pit, her body clad in newly made clothes, her belly full of the richest food. It was important that she represented the finest we could offer.

Again, you seem to sense us, and you glance towards the sky, a frown playing over your brow. The rising Moon is reflected in your eyes as you scan the narrow horizon above you, the disklike limits of your existence defined by the lips of the pit, a mirror of the Moon herself. Do you see us? I think not, but you do sense us, of that I am certain. And you are so like her, that one who went before. As alike as sisters. The same pale skin and raven hair, ice blue eyes so pale they are twins of the Moon.

In the woods behind us, an animal cries out in pain, caught by a night predator.

Something flickers through your eyes. Uncertainty, perhaps, or fear. Darkness has fallen, and you are alone in this place of death.

We, though, feel no such fear. We know this place of old. Far from the buried remains of our homes, liminal ground close by the stream, between field and hearth, a place not of the living, but of the spirits. A realm where men have no place. Only ghosts and the gods tread here without fear, and you are neither. We watch as you brush a tress of dark hair from your eyes, and then comes a flicker of alarm as the Moon emerges from behind a cloud. Do you see us in that moment, revealed in the Moon's light? I think you do, for your mouth opens, lips moving soundlessly as if you cannot believe what you are seeing. We step forward then, our toes touching the lip of the pit, and now we surround you from above, an unbroken ring.

A cycle. Endless.

Fear fills your eyes, but you should not be scared. This is how it ever was, how it ever must be. The earth must be renewed, the Moon placated so that the sun will rise again. We are the women of the village, and though our homes are long since gone, buried beneath the earth, this is our eternal task.

The first shovel-load of soil strikes your chest, and you stumble backwards. More wet clay is cast into the pit, heavy, blocky, and you struggle to regain your feet. The pit base is slippery, just as it was so many years ago when the first of you was placed here. You lose your footing, falling to the pit floor, and now we are heaping soil onto your legs, your torso, your arms, pinning you in your grave until only your face remains. Your eyes bulge in panic as you struggle to breathe, the weight of the soil compressing your lungs. But then the terror turns to realisation, and I watch you sink back onto your forever bed of clay. Your eyes meet mine, and across the millennia, we exchange a look of understanding.

As your face disappears beneath the next load of clay, I cast the stone onto your buried body. It will keep you from rising, ensure that your sacrifice is not in vain.

And year after year, the soil will yield its fruits, and we will watch, and we will wait: the women of the village, keeping you here beneath the fertile fields.

## AUTHOR NOTE

*I am a professional archaeologist, and the story above is based on Middle Bronze Age discoveries at several sites I have worked on. As to the existence of the watchers: then travel to those liminal places, those ancient and forgotten field edges by streams, far from village and town, and wait until the moon rises. They will come.*

# ELIZABETH R. MCCLELLAN
# THEIR EYES WERE WATCHING

Every night, between 1:15 and 1:30 am, the seer
dreams of the five-lobed burning eye
big as a world, iris iridescent no-color,
pupil spangled with spiral galaxies, peering

at them where they lay on their dented mattress.
The train blows its whistle two minutes later,
a relief, a thing of earth and iron, rattling
through the night as the seer gasps,

tries to breathe through their root mantra
until their heart stops jackrabbiting, the
adrenaline letdown shakes cease, leaves them
free to ponder *why*. They usually see mundane

events: weddings, births, heart attacks,
aneurysms, quinceañeras, bat mitzvot,
funerals and celebrations of life. Cassandra
is an instructive predecessor. Sees much,

.

says little, works their barista job for tips.
Every day they don't unload the bad news
is a gift, even if Luis on second shift is totally
freaked out by how they know who's going
to bail on their shift and who's just stuck
in traffic. They steam milk, whip cream,

## ELIZABETH R. MCCLELLAN
## THEIR EYES WERE WATCHING

block out the memory of the great eye
until one day they can't sleep, start Googling around.


No one has disclosed a similar visit.
They grow frantic, lost in the vision, stop sleeping,
lie awake in the dark looking for parallels,
Biblical angels, five-headed Brahma.


When that fails they find their courage,
try to stay in a few seconds more, up to
minutes, their dry eyes straining as they
stare into the great globe, asking *what, why,*


*explain, help*, get back only static and
snatches of music played on crystal flutes
over a satellite-slow heartbeat pulse. *Please.*
*Why are you here? Why this time? Why me?*


One Thursday in October the brown eyelids
close briefly over all five scorching lobes,
lashes thick as sequoia trunks, inflammable.
In that moment of respite the seer understands


too much, stifles a scream, nearly vomits,
understands deep in their gut why
*be not afraid* is the opener, wipes their face
with rosewater, goes outside to look at the moon
framed by branches, to feel dying grass under
their bare feet despite the chill. The moon blinks,
stares back. The seer screams, fingernails gouging face,
later led away sobbing *It comes! It comes!*

# ELEANOR GRAYDON
## SIN-EATER

I haunt my own body, a wraith of blood and bone. An echo of hunger, beating a drum against the ringing of my ribcage. Abandoned by everyone, including myself – a spectacle of caution and carrion. And like those scavengers, head bowed, I would eat for you.

Even as my stomach revolts, my throat tightens like a fist, every swallow tasting like ruin. I would let the meat rot as it moves down my throat, mourning as I devour. Wailing for the gods whose flesh I consume. Hollowing myself out as I tarnish their divinity with tongue and teeth. The taste turning to ash in my unworthy mouth.

I keen, between each wet sobbing breath that is drawn from overflowing lungs. Singing dirges in this increasingly bitter communion. Trading wafers and wine for marrow. Each bite a betrayal, each swallow, a prayer unanswered.

I mourn. Both you and I, the people we were before the hunger. Before this feast of shame and sanctity. Now, I am both holy and your grave. The weight of your bones and my lament sinking into freshly turned earth. Covered by things left alive, like so many swallowed sins.

# ALEXANDER SAXTON
## A SMALL LIGHT

It was a 'bright' asteroid; at the right angle, its hunched back of crystal, platinum and gold made it burn against the black sky like a distant sun.

It stretched more than thirty thousand feet across. It had been formed by a world-collision fourteen hundred million years before. Its silent path treaded once around the sun in sixty thousand years. It had worn this elliptic seven thousand (and four hundred) times.

From the star-watching rocks in northern Ontario (still warm with a faintness of the sun), a light-haired girl saw one of the stars shiver. But she had been crying, and she thought it was just a shiver from the tears in her eyes. She was lying on her back with thin arms folded across her belly. The night was growing cold. They'd been tears of rage, more than anything else. But there was so much to be enraged about. And now, now that the anger had burned away, its residue was black and silent inside her.

The asteroid turned. Its shining half faced away from the sun, and for a while the rock flew dark. Burning sunlight drained from its frozen landscape, leaving tessellations of shadow.

A bare foot touched down upon the stone; a second one hovered momentarily, then settled down beside it. A man surveyed the black land; the frozen stone; the veins of metal fading red to leaden-grey as they lost the sun's heat. He was dressed in gold brocade and strings of sapphire. His eyes were a sort of faded blue, like if the sky was painted on with old enamel. His hair and wings were gold. His skin didn't burn from radiation; his blood didn't freeze from cold; and the liquids of his brain didn't boil from vacuum. He was quite serene.

He knelt. As he'd known they would, the palms of his long and well-made hands found a deep cranny in the stone. So many cycles of heat-and-cold-and-heat-and-cold, even the hardest protoplanetary rock would split. He placed his hands in this wound, thoughtfully, as if he could feel the asteroid's pain, and then slowly grounded his feet on black enstatite. He looked down, and gave the great satellite a look of such gentle remorse. Then he unfolded his body.

There can be no sound in endless vacuum. But a rumble of agonized rock ran up through the soles of his feet and out to the golden pinions of his wings; that groan echoed through his bones and tendons, to the hammer-anvil-stirrup of the inner ear. He trembled with the stones' pain. And then the asteroid broke. Like a knee-cap smashed with a sledgehammer, the crust of gold and crystal ripped away from its home of a billion years. The two shards of planetoid hurtled away from one another; and the great wrenching change of speed and vector should have hurled the Angel into space. But his bare feet lay steady on the rock as if planted on the sun-warmed stones of north Ontario. Crystal, gold and platinum cracked loose, ripping free with the sudden surge of centrifugal force. They passed from the asteroid's shadow, and burst into brilliant light.

For a moment, from the star-watching rocks, it was as if a new star had bloomed; and the light-haired girl sat up, catching her breath; forgetting everything in momentary wonder.

Then the cloud dispersed, and the new star faded out, and the light on the girl's face dimmed once more. She watched the heavens for some second sign, but nothing came. She wiped her face and looked back down at earth; at the black trees and black water underneath her rocky tor. She shivered. It had gotten later than she'd realized—and colder, too.

When the glittering shards had whipped into darkness behind him, the Angel spread his wings and rose on the strength of a single step, to land again where gold and crystal had once been heaped. As he folded his wings, the asteroid came back round to the sun, and he turned his gaze up to the obliterating light. It was a light that showed his bones right through him, but he looked into it as if into the cool skies of a spring afternoon. It was a hard, clean light. It burned in all directions. After his eyes had been sated, he let his gaze drift from the glory of the sun, toward the slim blue planet (sapphire crescent; small enough to pinch between his thumb and finger) that showed back its light. His face was carven, hieratic. It was a face for solemnity, and when it smiled, the expression bordered on obscene. But he smiled, and bent to one knee and rested his palms on the matte black stone. He closed his pale blue eyes, and *felt* the black asteroid tumble down its new trajectory, unseen.

Far below, a girl with pale hair walked down from the star-watching rocks with hands in pockets. A cold wind was blowing in the pine boughs, and it made stars shimmer on the surface of the flat black tarn. Her boots crunched on the gravel path. She wasn't happy now, but found herself at least at peace.

One way or another, things would come out right.

# ANGELIKA MAY
# TELLING THE BEES

God beckoned man to Him, and encouraged Adam to perch atop His knee. Adam settled at the summit, letting his legs dangle, his heels occasionally knocking God's colossal tibia, the impact as inconsequential as a leaf landing upon a shoulder. Together they gazed upon the fell across the barren side of Eden.

God broke their unified awestruck silence with a theatrical demonstration—with a snap of His fingers, the fell sprang to life. Animals were conjured, flora burst into prismatic hues, fauna blossomed, swelling to grotesque proportions. God conceived a rill, parted its lips, and asked the mouth to meet the sea. With glass particles hidden in His jet, He manifested sand and created a beach. He lifted the waves toward the sky and bade them kiss, causing the stars to sink into the water. "Salt", He named this miracle, and declared it good.

God directed His attention back to Adam, His homunculus, made in His own likeness. Cradling him in His palm, He gazed into the core of Adam's earthly body. Within Adam's chest lay a hollow where a heart should have been. God placed a hand upon His own chest but was met with silence, rather than a rhythmic beating. There had been a beat before the conception of Adam.

God caused Adam to sleep, and from his side He tore forth a woman, severing the muscles and tendons that encased her in a sac. She emerged vibrant, like a sprightly cervid creature, her essence imbued with an ancient understanding. God used His tongue to wipe the blood, which was matted in her tresses. Afterwards, he sewed Adam shut using a filament of her hair.

When Adam awoke, he tried to name her Woman, but God called her Eve.

The hollow in Adam's chest still troubled God, so He devised a task to test him, to determine whether humanity could still exhibit care without a heart. He could not destroy man, he was not yet so wrathful, there were no locusts hidden in His Egyptian cotton pockets, but it grieved Him that Adam had been created imperfectly.

"At the edge of Eden lies a hive," God instructed. "Its bees are the lifeblood of this garden. Without their labour, Eden will wither, and you will perish. You must inform the bees of every birth, death, and union. They thrive on knowing the stories of others; it is their purpose, and through it, they sustain the world."

God would secretly sacrifice Himself, with the condition that if Adam informed the bees of His passing, humanity would be spared; but if Adam failed, humanity would face certain destruction. Adam turned away with a scoff, and God watched him retreat toward the eastern side.

Sorrow descended over God, dimming His radiant halo. Wandering through Eden, dragging His feet, He was filled with such anxious trepidation that He almost vomited from the fear of impending death. To quell His shaking hands, God spontaneously plucked eight poisonous berries from a thorny bush—enough to slay a deity. With quiet resignation, He consumed them, one by one, all too quickly, overcome with such urgent self-deprecation. Foolish God, He thought, eager God who created a mirror image wrong. Upon ingesting the berries, He was met with a sour, rancid taste as the berries burned painfully against His stomach acid.

The symptoms began. Soon, God became nauseous and dizzy, His heart beating like an ancient sacrificial drum. He lay down and clutched His own stomach, wishing for a mother. As the toxins spread, He was overtaken by an intense cramp, briefly relieved by vomit that splurged out the side of His mouth, how embarrassing. In this agony, He cursed Adam, His errant son, for all the pain expelling from His body, for making a God helpless. I am alone, He thought. There will be no one to close My eyelids after I am gone.

In the final stages, the venom caused His limbs to become immobile, and a cold numbness crept over His body. Dimming, everything is dimming. His breathing grew shallow, irregular. He begged for an antidote, but it was no use. As His strength waned, He called out to Adam with His final breath, "Where art thou?" From His lips came a single honeybee, which flew to Eve and whispered of His passing, along with the task that had been entrusted to Adam.

While hunting, Adam was struck by a searing pain in his stomach. He slithered back toward the eastern side, adder-like. Along the way, earthworms emerged from their soil, they turned to face him and spoke in unison, "Your heart lies in your stomach," they hissed, "and its beating is troubling us."

Upon his return, Eve delivered the news of God's passing with great solemnity. She turned away from Adam, mourning in silence, regretting that she had not been chosen as the earth's keeper to carry out the task herself.

She urged Adam to fulfil God's command and inform the bees of His death. Throwing a black shroud to him, she said:

'Take this and cover the hive. Tell the bees—those flying in and out—of one who has taken the journey we all must take. Move the hive slightly to the right to signify change, ensuring the entrance faces the gates of Eden. Speak to the bees in hushed tones; they are delicate and easily disturbed. Change unsettles them, causing them to tear pollen from their bodies in fear. They'll be too frightened to eat or work. Knock once on each hive, then tell them, "Our God is dead and gone." This should be done at midnight, or better still, if sung and rhymed:

'Bees, oh bees, awake and hear,
Our Lord has passed, the end is near.
We come to tell, in a mournful tone,
The keeper's gone, you're not alone.'
Wait for them to buzz—it's a good omen."

Adam, burdened by the pain in his stomach, refused, he would not be responsible for God' passing. "I can't", he muttered. Days turned into weeks. Eve, too, had been made wrong.

God had poured too much forgiveness into her, saturating her soul with an overabundance of love, empathy, and kindness. These gifts compelled her to accept Adam's pain as a rightful excuse for his ineptitude, one she had never been allowed. She nurtured him not as an equal, but as a mother tending to a wayward child. Her hands would gently rub his stomach in solace, whilst her head urged her to strike him across the face for his relentless indolence.

Each morning, Eve laid lilies on God's resting place and begged the bees for patience. Each evening Eve would coax Adam's heavy body to move, sitting him up to be nourished with the food she had foraged, hunted, killed, seasoned and roasted. Afterwards, she would carry him to the stream to be washed, and nearly succumb to the weight of his body. The water ran in rivulets down her lover's form, as despair coursed through hers, she knew that her unwavering willingness to care for him would be their undoing, yet resisting him was impossible. Adam's beauty, his radiant presence, made tending to him feel like a reward. Her hands lingered on his clammed, sickly, aching skin. However, the incessant buzzing of bees filled her ears, "stop," she whispered to the bees, "let him rest."
Love betrays her.

As Eve bent over him, Adam felt the weight of his own helplessness. His thoughts fleeted between the garden, and the duty that God had entrusted with him. How had it come to this? How am I now languid in the arms of a woman? The guilt however, soon dissipated and Adam surrendered to her indulgences; it was too easy to be cared for by another.

Weakened by neglect, the bees swarmed in desperation, their humming swelling through the air like a thunderclap. They descended upon God's body, a black tide of restless motion and stirred life back into Him. God awoke, His grief transmuted into vengeance.

"Men who eat bread are a plague; you are cursed above all cattle and beasts of the field. You shall eat dust, and I will multiply humanity's sorrow. Every child conceived will suffer pain for generations, and their lives will be cruel. Sickness will afflict them, and they will toil in misery, aging too quickly. The earth, sky, and sea will overflow with evils. Diseases will haunt humanity day and night, and I will send them suffering"

The bees by the hand of God turned on Adam, black cluster, black hounds, Baskerville. Pom! Pom!

They burrowed into his flesh, replacing his veins with honey and his heart with a hive until Adam became nothing more than a buzzing shadow.

Eve woke to a man with honeycomb eyes.

The bees tore through the earth.

They gathered as a dense, fuzzy fist at the end of Adam's wrist, ready to strike thy neighbor. They coalesced around his groin, morphing into a pulsating, throbbing form. They reformed into fingers, tearing at the skirts of women who fled in terror. They constructed themselves into a shaft, a pistol, and two humming hands to fire a shot between the eyes of the poorest child. They ripped the bread from the mouths of the child's siblings. They gathered as a billowing cloud of smog, choking anyone who inhaled their scopal hairs. They joined as moustaches beneath the noses of murderous men. They enveloped Palestine, leaving a black

void on the map. They soared to the sea, launching their dark bodies onto the waves, turning the water onyx. Some transformed into the stalk, the cap, the base, and a rare few took the shape of the gills of a radioactive mushroom. They dropped onto civilians and houses, encased as tight, round steel shells, and surged as smoke from the collateral damage. They spilled out from bodies, from wounds, black blood, and carried the bodies away in black body bags.

The earth was suspended in devastation and God could do nothing but turn his back, resign and appoint Eve as mother to all that dwell upon the earth. And so, while Adam continued his rampage, Eve tended to the wounded, binding the injuries of those Adam had struck, sewing new skirts for the women who had fled in terror, burying the child who had fallen. She fed the surviving siblings, blew the choking clouds of smog away, and rescued those she could, carrying them to safety from the murderous men. She clung to memory, marking the places that should not be forgotten. She worked tirelessly to dilute the poisoned waters, tried to suck the radiation from the afflicted bodies, rebuilding homes where she could, and marking the graves of those who had been carried away.

From her pocket, she released a lone honeybee, dogged in its determination it made its way toward a single flower that bloomed amidst the wreckage.

# ANONYMOUS
# FELO DE SE

A man he played the fiddle
Upon a rib cage exposed
A man he promised eternity
Upon a broken road
"Such secrets I have for you"
He promised every time
Please no I beg of you
A corpse is dragged down

Crossroads drown through sorrow
A curse buried in the soil
They took away his family
Burned through his estate
Now he stands before you broken
Decayed and twisted of mind
Rotten garments sway to a breeze
Full of stench and threat

Yet he chunners all their secrets
Tales from a world underneath
Where skin is flayed away
And screams are strangled
Where no dreams outlast nightmares
And souls find no reprieve only judgment

He lay in the fires down there
With one eye on his road
The road you now find yourself
Lost, betrayed and broken
Exhaustion sways you greatly

## ANONYMOUS
## FELO DE SE

Mirrored by the ghoul below
Rooted to the spot you cry
But alone is all you will find

The fiddle shrieks like gales
While the mud grabs your knees
You dance entwined with the devil
Screaming mercy, shouting pleas
Earth to your chest then your neck
A deserted road so cruel
A sob muffled by soil
Is the only promise you'll know

# ANONYMOUS
# BRACKEN

I heard you laughing in the woods, but I'm glad I didn't see. When the leaves swayed for your entrance, I turned and ran away.

# ABOUT THE AUTHORS

## VANESSA SANTOS
*Vanessa Santos was born and raised on a tiny island in the middle of the Atlantic. She now lives in Scotland (though still by the sea) and spends as much of her time as possible devouring stories, writing stories, and wandering the endless Scottish woods. Her short fiction has been published online at Samjoko Magazine and Idle Ink, and in anthologies by Sliced Up Press, Colp, and Solar Press. Her debut collection 'MAKE A HOME OF ME' is being published in 2025 by Dead Ink Press. You can follow her adventures on Instagram: @nesscbsantos*

## FLORENCE-SUSANNE REPPERT
*Florence-Susanne Reppert is an ex-Lehigh Valley resident and currently resides in Monroe County. They run/own Poetry as Promised Literary Magazine and Cohost Nowhere as Promised Open Mic in Allentown PA. They are a Photographer, Poet, Parent, and lover of sloths. You can follow them everywhere except in real life under schizo_trash_poet*

## AMY BOUCHER
*Amy Boucher is a writer and folklorist, who focuses on her native Shropshire. Her emphasis is primarily on the interplay between folklore, history and the paranormal, and perceptions of the past through the lens of folk beliefs. She has written a folk horror audio drama about Shropshire's satanic folk tales.*
*You can find Amy's blog at nearlyknowledgeablehistory.blogspot.com*

## LYDIA WAITES
*Lydia Waites is a Yorkshire based writer and Creative Writing PhD candidate at the University of Lincoln, specialising in short fiction and folklore. She is a Fiction Editor for The Lincoln Review and her work has appeared in The Baltimore Review, Door Is a Jar, Streetcake Magazine, Porridge Magazine, York Literary Review, The Abandoned Playground and more.*

*You can find Lydia on Twitter @waies_lydia, Bluesky*
*@lydiawaites.bsky.social and @lydiawaieswrites on Instagram.*

## ADAM HASSAN
*Pint sized 40 year old Renegade Poet and part-time Rebel Rock Star.*
*Fanatical music aficionado with a particular taste for 1960's*
*Psychedelia and other various styles. Former Social Policy student*
*specialising in Radical Left Wing Libertarian Politics . Avid reader of*
*the Gothic, Romantic, Dystopian, Utopian, Surrealist and Erotic, to*
*name just a handful of the genres he enjoys. Decadent glugger of*
*Champagne and other mainly sparkling wines but anything he can*
*drink which his body can take. He has had some of his poetry published*
*before in the Surrealist magazine 'Patastrophe, his main influences are*
*Blake, Byron, Shelley, Keats, Donne, Coleridge, Caroll, Poe, Rossetti,*
*Baudelaire, Rochester, Cooper Clarke, and of course, Shakespeare.*

## C.J SUBKO
*C.J. Subko is a dreamer and a dabbler. She has a Ph.D. in Clinical*
*Psychology from Michigan State University and a B.A. in Psychology*
*and English from the University of Notre Dame, which makes her*
*highly qualified to think too much. Her short fiction publications*
*include Die Laughing (October 2024), Small Wonders (November*
*2024), Morgana le Fay (Flame Tree Press; March 2025), The*
*Deadlands (April 2025), and an upcoming issue of Penumbric*
*Speculative Fiction. She is a member of the HWA and SFWA. Her*
*novels are represented by Maria Brannan at Greyhound Literary*
*Agency. She can be found at www.cjsubko.com.*

## LINDA BROMILOW
*Linda Bromilow is a busy mother of nobody. Her hobbies include*
*quaffing champagne, idling and reading questionable novels.*
*Changeling.*

## ALI MALONEY
*Ali Maloney was raised with video nasties in the news and Batman*
*licensed as a breakfast cereal... and it shows. He is fascinated with the*
*idea of stories themselves being haunted — and the very act of reading*
*them as being part of the ritual described.*

*A trained clown and sometime noise-rapper, he has performed on stages as diverse as T In The Park and the Sonic Arts Expo in Plymouth; from live sessions on New York's top alternative radio station, WFMU, to Edinburgh and Glasgow Horror Festivals. His theatre shows include the bleak panto of RATCATCHER and the diluvial romp of HYDRONOMICON. Currently, he co-hosts the weird art cabaret, ANATOMY, and runs the urban wyrd horror podcast, CALEDONIAN GOTHIC. "Brilliant." - BBC Radio Scotland. You can find Ali on Bluesky @alimaloney.bsky.social*

## LAURA CATHCART

*Laura Cathcart works under the name Cut Fingers, and is one-half of the Infested Publishing team. Her artwork is inspired by and immersed in the eerie realms of horror movies, English folklore, and death metal. She occasionally writes surrealist poetry, exploring themes of mortality, religious trauma and the supernatural, inviting readers to confront the unsettling aspects of existence.*

*Her poems "LXXXIX" and "Ashen Humanity" were published in the "Surrealaerpool" magazine 'Patastrophe! (2022).*

*Laura was raised by a strong familial unit of working class women in a town decimated by cuts, which has instilled in her a sense of perseverance and resilience.*

*You can find her on Twitter @_cutfingers*

## AMANDA BLAKE

*A mass of tentacles and rose vines masquerading as a person, Amanda M. Blake is the author of such horror titles as QUESTION NOT MY SALT, DEEP DOWN, and OUT OF CURIOSITY AND HUNGER, dark poetry collection DEAD ENDS, and the Thorns fairy tale mash-up series. For more, visit amandamblake.com.*

## STEPHEN HOWARD

*Stephen Howard (he/him) is an English novelist and short story writer from Manchester, now living in Cheshire with his wife, Rachel, and their daughter, Flo. An English Literature and Creative Writing graduate from the Open University, his work has been published by Lost Boys Press, The No Sleep Podcast, Metastellar, and others. He's also published one novel, a comic fantasy titled Beyond Misty Mountain, and the collections Condemned To Be, Little Book of*

*Horrors, & Ophelia in the Underworld and Other Melancholy Tales
(Alien Buddha Press, 2023). A horror novella is forthcoming from Wild
Hunt Books in 2025. Find Stephen at:
Twitter: @SteJHoward
TikTok: @SteJHoward
Website: www.stephenhowardblog.wordpress.com*

## ADAM HULSE

*Adam Hulse's debut 'the Tales of Tupuqa' three novella horror series
was published by Raven Tale Publishing in 2021. His poem "The
Summit" made Punk Noir Magazines "21 Essential Punk Noir Stories
and Poems" list for the same year.
Adam's flash fiction and short stories feature in highly successful
anthologies "206 Word Stories Horror", "Something Bad Happened",
"A 3-B Halloween", Sinister Stories By The Ten", and "The Nightmare
Never Ends".
May 2023 saw the release of his dystopian horror novella "Below
Economic Thresholds" (3-B Publishing), while his debut horror/sci-fi
collection "Not A Good Fit At This Time" (Infested Publishing) was
also released in 2023.
The Growth Ultimate Edition was released through Infested Publishing
in 2023, with sci-fi/alternative history novella 'The Forgotten War'
released early 2025.
Adam is raising two strong daughters in an underfunded small town in
the North West of England.*

## SASHA RAVITCH

*Sasha (she/her) is an author, educator, consultant, and critic on the
subjects of Cosmic Horrors (real/imagined), and the ecstatic-grotesque
of the body (monster-flesh, the witchbody, chronic illness and body
dysmorphia) in (Oc)culture, Literature, and Film. She professionally
consults on aforementioned matters, presents at conferences, and
writes film and literary criticism on these subjects. She has been
published by Hadean Press and Asteria Press, with forthcoming fiction
in Cosmic Horror Monthly, Bloodletter Magazine, Cursed Morsels
Press, and Neither Fish Nor Foul. When not creating for Patreon,
Substack, or MovieJawn, she teaches The Red Flesh Workshops, writes
weird stories exploring the intersection of outer space and the body,
and is a*

*Speculative Fiction editor for Lumina Literary journal.*

## WIEBO GROBLER
*Born in South Africa and raised in a small farming community, Wiebo only had his imagination to keep him occupied, til he discovered the magic of books.*
*He fell in love with the characters within from an early age. Soon he began to create his own worlds and stories in his head. These stories developed voices, which clamored to be heard. So, he writes. Shortlisted for his Flash Fiction and Poetry for the Fish Publishing Prize he had various stories published in Molotov Lit, National Flash Fiction Day, Reflex Fiction, and more.*
*Twitter: @Wiebog*
*Bluesky: wiebo.bsky.social*

## DAVID MITCHELL
*David Kenneth Mitchell is a fledgling author from Cornwall, England. He was inspired to pick up the pen again - for the first time since school - by Michelle Paver's Dark Matter, and was recently published in Speculation Publication's Grimm Retold. He enjoys the weird and wonderful, and playing with and subverting well used tropes.*

## RYAN DAY
*Ryan resides in Derby, UK, primarily writing in the horror and fantasy genres. He has previously self-published a series of horror novellas as well as having short genre stories featured in publications by Red Cape Press, Spiral Tower Press and Unsettling Reads.*

## J D M YODER
*J.D.M Yoder is a queer, non-binary writer from northeast Ohio currently working as a pharmacy technician. Growing up in the countryside has given them a love for the natural world, and the myriad of books read out on the back porch left them with an endless desire to create. You can find them on Twitter @jdmyoder*

## JONATHAN HART
*Jonathan is a professional archaeologist who loves the otherness of the past, something that informs his stories. As well as writing, he enjoys long-distance and ultra running, which gives him plenty of time to*

*dream up new stories and fix plot holes! He volunteers as a Squirrel Scout leader, where story telling around fires is part of our DNA. He lives in the Cotswolds with his wife and five daughters, all of whom are keen readers. You can find him on twitter @JontyHart01*

## ELIZABETH R. MCCLELLAN

*Elizabeth R. McClellan is a white disabled gender/queer neurospicy demisexual lesbian poet writing on unceded Quapaw and Chikshaka Yaki land. Kan work has appeared in many venues, including Strange Horizons, Nightmare Magazine, and fwp 2024: an anthology of queer writing. Ka is a past recipient of the Judy Neri Scholarship for Disabled Poets, the Naked Girls Reading Literary Honors Award, and a past Rhysling Award Finalist. Ka can be found on social media as popelizbet (primarily Bluesky), on patreon as ermcclellan, or at the ever evolving popelizbet.com.*

## ELEANOR GRAYDON

*Eleanor Graydon is a University Student, Freelance Editor and Poet, based in Queensland Australia. Her work has previously appeared in Wireworm Magazine's second issue (2023), Litmora Magazine's fourth issue: Ecohorror (2024), WILDsound Writing festival (2024), AZE Journal (2025), and Wireworm Magazine's third Issue (2025). You can find Eleanor on Instagram: @sleepingeurydice, Bluesky: @sleepingeurydice.bsky.social, and Twitter (X): @sleep_eurydice.*

## ALEXANDER SAXTON

*Alexander Saxton writes fiction and crawls around like a rat repairing draught beer equipment in the bar basements of Toronto, Canada. He's the co-showrunner of WRONG STATION, a podcast anthology of original horror and weird short stories (wherever fine podcasts are dispensed or extruded.) You can find him on socials at @aewsaxton.bsky.social, and you can find some little games he's designed at https://she-wolf-productions.itch.io.*

## ANGELIKA-MAY

*Angelika May is a 25-year-old half-Polish, half-English working class writer and actor from Bradford, based in London. Angelika works in a vast scope of media; in film she has co-authored a short film alongside BAFTA crew writer/director Ana Pio on feminist politics and sexual assault, '7 to 10', and is working her second short, written in both English and Polish titled 'Dobranoc' (Goodnight), that delves into the theme of loss of culture and grief, with director Aleksandra Czenczek. In theatre, she has authored two plays, 'The Unicorn In Captivity', staged in July 2024 and 'A Murder of Crows', in its final development. Angelika's poem 'Holy' was shortlisted for the 2024 Heroica poetry prize and published in their first anthology, 'Body Odyssey' and had three poems, 'Pasture', 'Mama' and 'SCUM' published by BASH Magazine. Angelika is currently working on her first long-form novel and short story collection. Outside of creative writing, Angelika works as a music journalist, she is the editor of Hideous Mag and writes for publications such as DAZED, DIY and Hard of Hearing, covering the dynamic grassroots scene in London. You can find her on Instagram @angiefrombradford and her portfolio at https://www.clippings.me/angelikamay*

## ANONYMOUS POET

*Anonymous is a shadow lingering just behind the candlelight. No birth, no death, only scrawled reveries and contemplations left beneath moss-laden rocks for us to find. We may not know their face, but we have heard their voice – in the vast ocean waves crashing against soft white sands, the oppressive forests that emits more dark than light, and cold concrete alleyways, soaked in the orange glow that we swear we heard hum our name.*

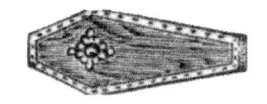

*Working-class publishers based in the North-West of England, with a mission to amplify the voices of working-class writers; creating a platform for stories that challenge, inspire, and disrupt the norm.*

*Specialising in horror, sci-fi, speculative, and gothic fiction.*

**Other releases by Infested Publishing:**

Too Bad You Died: An Infested Publishing Anthology
The Forgotten War by Adam Hulse
Never Leaving by Elford Alley
Stories Christians Don't Have to Read Backwards by Damien Casey

**Upcoming release:** Sins of My Sisters – J V Gachs

**www.infestedpublishing.com**
**infested.publishing@gmail.com**

Printed in Dunstable, United Kingdom